A BRUGEL FAIRYTALE
TREASURY

Far-fetched fables

EBONY MCKENNA

Dedication

For the long-suffering Brugelese;
constantly overlooked throughout history,
the Eurovision Song Contest and map production.

Please note that this collection of fairytales is written using Brugelish English spelling and will therefore differ from US or UK English in that regard.

#LoveOzYA

CONTENTS

What and Where is Brugel?

(Source: Brugelwiki.org.bu)

BRUGEL (pron. Broo-gl) Officially: The Serene Duchy of Brugel. Brugel is a small country in Eastern Europe. It is the only country in the world with a hexagonal flag. It has a single house of parliament, the Dentate (the place with teeth).

The First Minister is the head of government. The Duke of Brugel is the head of state.

Brugel is at the crossroads of old and new Europe. Previously part of the USSR, Brugel declared independence in 1991 and shares its northern and eastern borders with Slaegal, its western and southern borders with Craviç and holds on with its fingertips to an acreage of beach along The Black Sea. The capital and largest city is Venzelemma.

The Brugel language is derived from an earlier form of English. This came about after many Jutes,

Angles and Saxons took a wrong turn in the fifth century and found themselves at the Black Sea. [Citation needed]

Brugel has survived through many hardships, having been annexed into the Constantine, Austro-Hungarian, Prussian and Holy Roman empires at various – and mercifully short – times in history. In the 1950s Soviet tanks often rumbled through the main streets of Venzelemma – on their way to somewhere else.

Any rumours you may have heard about Brugel are probably true. All psychics and mediums can trace their DNA to the foothills of Brugel. The countryside is the birthplace of far-fetched folklore and fairytales. Talking animals are interwoven into daily life. This is a country where the strange and unusual are not only tolerated, they are encouraged.

The First Champion Snowgoat

With such brutally cold winters, most of Brugel's wildlife cope in two ways:
hibernating or taking a hike. The species that do remain have evolved to grow
thick winter coats to protect against arctic north winds, rain, sleet, hail and the
twenty-three kinds of snow. The thickest coat belongs to the snowgoat, a native
to Eastern Europe.

O ne horribly cold winter afternoon, a farmer called Petrov was out in the snow, checking his traps. To his surprise and delight, there was an especially large and heavy-coated snowgoat hanging by its back leg in a tree. The snowgoat would feed his family for at least a week, and the thick coat would make warm clothes for his growing children.

He approached the snowgoat with an axe.

"Nooooo!" The snowgoat bleated. "Don't kill me!"

Petrov held his axe and said, "I'm sorry, but I have

to. I have a hungry and cold family. Your meat will feed us and your skin will keep us warm."

"Then we have a conflict," said the snowgoat. "I need my skin covering me to stay warm and stay alive. I'll happily share my oats and dandelions with you instead, to fill your belly. I have a cave not far from here, where it's out of the weather."

At which point Petrov scratched his head and said, "Knock me sideways and call me late for dinner, a talking snowgoat!"

"Yes, That too!" said the snowgoat. "I'm a talking goat and that makes me special, so you can't kill me. You need me as proof that goats can talk, otherwise all your friends will think you're broken."

Petrov scratched his head again. "I'm really cold, and I'm really hungry, and I'm really, *really* tired. I'm not sure I'm making good life choices at this point. Talking or not, I'm still hungry and cold and it's a long way back down the hills to my farm. How do we resolve this?"

"Cut me loose first, and we can work it out."

"You're not just trying to trick me?"

The snowgoat scoffed. "Course not! I'll help you get home faster. It's mostly downhill from here, yeah? We can slide down."

"Are you sure this isn't a trick?" Petrov asked.

"N-noooooo, never." The snowgoat said. "But I am upside down and all the blood is rushing to my head. Be a dear and cut the rope?"

Petrov cut the rope and the snowgoat fell down onto the snow. He took a few moments to get back on his feet – or hooves to be more precise.

The snowgoat said, "I gave you my word that I wouldn't run off after you cut me down, so now I will keep my word and help you get home quickly. My name's Galyna, by the way. Nice to meet you."

"Petrov," Petrov said. "And, Galyna's a girls' name, isn't it?"

Galyna snapped back, "Are you making fun of me?"

"No, never!"

Galyna the snowgoat had long horns that curled in a majestic arc around his head. To Petrov's surprise, Galyna rolled onto his back and planted his horns into the snow like runners. Then he tucked his legs and hooves into his chest and began sliding down the hill.

"Wait for me!" Petrov called out.

Galyna rolled onto his side and waited until Petrov reached him. Then he said, "Climb on!"

Petrov sat on Galyna's upturned tummy.

Galyna said, "If you face forward, you can see which way we're going, and you can steer us in the right direction."

"Hey, that's a great idea!"

The two of them, with some teamwork, slid down the hills all the way to the farmhouse.

What a rush!

"One more thing," Galyna said. "When we get to

your farmhouse, maybe it's best you don't tell them I can talk."

"But why? It's what makes you special. You'll be famous. Wait a moment, *I'll* be famous."

"I'm shy." Galyna said. "And people get weird when they find out I can talk. They want to have in-depth discussions with me, and find solutions to all the world's problems. I never went to school, I don't know what they're talking about. And don't even get me started with politics! I'm a goat, not a guru!"

"But, you're a talking goat! That's amazing!"

"Yes, and you're a talking human. If you don't mind me being blunt, you're hardly the sparkling conversationalist yourself."

"Point taken."

Petrov the Farmer took the goat to show the family. "My darling family, what we have here is a most remarkable goat."

Galyna bleated goatfully and gave Petrov the side-eye, just to make sure Petrov kept his word.

Petrov announced to his family, "This is a unique sliding goat, and he is amazing. We can get down from the hills so much faster, using him as a sled. It will make our winter work so much easier. And when we're not working, I'm sure we could create rides in the snow for the children."

Petrov's wife smiled gleefully at the goat. "Are you sure we can't give him a trim and knit some jumpers out of all that wool? He'll still get to keep his skin."

Galyna bleated goatfully again and nudged Petrov with his horns.

"He needs the thick coat to slide in the snow properly. Come outside children, let us show the neighbours what this incredible goat can do."

For the next few days, Galyna and the children played in the snow - which was pretty excellent as it meant they weren't in the house, getting underfoot.

Then something very special happened. The neighbourhood children also came outdoors into the snow and took it in turns to ride Galyna. Soon, they were placing bets on who was the fastest down the hill, who made the best jumps (Galyna wasn't a fan of the jumping part, it hurt his back) and who did the most spectacular dismounts.

Within two weeks, they had an entire competition sorted out, complete with rules and regulations, distances, times and leaderboards.

They went into the hills and convinced more snowgoats to join in the fun. The snowgoats were delighted to have somewhere warm to stay the night, with plenty of food and water. They didn't mind that they spent their days taking children for rides, because they were pretty light to carry. They only grew tired when the adults wanted rides. The adults weren't as good as the children at the dismounts or steering, so they soon grew tired of the games.

The children of Brugel were excited to have started something that made their horrible winters that much more bearable. If anything, it gave them something to look forward to in the few hours of daylight during those cold end-of-year months.

The competitions became so fast and fierce, people became concerned about accidents and falls. Bloodstains in the snow are so offputting! The children opted to wear helmets. Then many also added kneepads, elbow pads and some began to wear strong leathers all over.

Galyna tutted and muttered when he and Petrov were in private.

"The children look silly wearing helmets," Galyna said after a particularly strenuous afternoon of snow-goating.

Petrov shrugged, "Silly or not, it is good for their safety."

"It gives them a false sense of safety and they're not paying attention. Brugel is becoming a nanny-goat state!"

And that is how the particularly Brugelish sport of snowgoating came to be. It's also why snowgoats these days have been selectively bred to have exceptionally curly horns, as these are essential to good snowgoating race times.

Petrov kept Galyna's secret and never told anyone, to protect his privacy but also because he wasn't sure he really wanted Galyna to share his bizarre views with a wider audience.

Decades later, the truth came to light. One day, after his grandchildren had exhausted themselves snowgoating on the hills, they came home to sit by the fire. One of them looked at the books above the mantelpiece and selected one to read.

It was her grandfather Petrov's diary.

"Grandfather, could Galyna really talk?"

"Yes, poppet, he could."

"What did he talk about?"

"He was an odd one, for sure. He thought the rules of snowgoating were fixed to favour smaller goats and that he was being discriminated against because of his age."

"That's rather odd."

"Indeed. He was hardly the *bon vivant*. He had some weird ideas. He said the Grand Duke of Brugel and the royal family were really lizards disguised as humans, and that the earth was flat. But to be honest I have no idea what he was bleating on about."

"Gosh, what a shame. I'd had rather high esteem for Galyna up until now."

Petrov hugged his granddaughter. "We can remember him for the fun we had, and perhaps learn to curb our own weirdness later in life, which could otherwise tarnish our legacies."

"That's very sensible, Grandfather."

"You see why we need to keep his secret. It was amazing that he could talk, but what he talked about was mostly rubbish. Best we remember him as the first champion snowgoat, and the creator of our unique national sport."

The granddaughter closed the diary and put it back on the shelf. "Grandfather, I think we put too much value on the ability to talk, rather than the ability to invent fun things."

"You're very wise, Poppet. Talking is overrated."

The family kept the secret of Galyna's ability to talk. Whenever the topic came up, they emphasised Galyna's achievements and actions.

Which is why everybody today understands that actions are so much more valuable than words.

Three Princesses of Serendy

ONE OF THE FIRST RECORDED FAIRYTALES IN
THE WORLD, ACCORDING TO BRUGELORE

A very long time long ago, before even your parents were born, there lived three princesses on the island of Serendy.

Their mother was a great and powerful Queen called Gif. Most people said her name with a hard G like Gift and Give, but others said it with a soft G like Ginger and Giraffe. The three princesses all called her Mummy in private, and Your Majesty in public, which didn't help matters at all.

Anyway, Queen Gif wanted her three daughters to have the very best education possible. This would not only set them up in the future, but also reflect marvellously on Queen Gif to have three such clever daughters.

Queen Gif scoured the lands for the very best teachers to come to the palace and instruct her daughters, which was excellent for the princesses, but a bit rough on the schools who missed their most talented staff.

After three years of intensive instruction, the princesses were all examined for their prowess in languages, mathematics, science and art. The Queen was delighted.

She announced, "I'm so proud of how intelligent you are, I can now abdicate the throne to you."

But the princesses were loving their education, and didn't want to stop.

"We are still only half as clever as you, and there are three of us, so in effect we are each only one sixth as clever as you."

The mathematics classes had clearly paid off.

Instead of being happy, Queen Gif cracked the sads. "I've devoted my life to ruling, now I want some time off. Surely the three of you could take it in turns?"

The three princesses sensed a trap – Mummy must be testing them, to see how greedy they were for the throne. By declining to take it, they were able to prove they could be trusted. At least, that's what they hoped.

Playing psychological games with monarchs was always fraught!

Queen Gif threw her hands in the air and said, "Fine then, I'll keep working. Also, you've all been accepted to the University of Beramo. Off you go then, have fun and study hard."

On the way to university, the three princesses were curious about whether they were indeed clever enough to secure a place, or whether their family name and enormous wealth had opened doors for them.

"How will we ever know if we qualified on merit?" One Princess asked.

Another responded, "That is a difficult question. I feel I am clever enough, but perhaps I lack self-awareness and I truly am not that smart?"

The third said, "Only somebody with self-awareness would question their lack of self-awareness."

The first said, "A condundrum for sure."

The second said, "Conundrums confuse me."

The third said, "We may have answered our question."

No sooner had they enrolled in university than the dean of Beramo asked them into his office. "On your journey here, did you encounter any animal tracks?"

"Yes, we did." One of the princesses said. "We saw hoofmarks in the gravel. But only three strong marks, the fourth was soft. I can only assume it was lame."

The second said, "It was a goat, because of the size of the hoof marks. It was a very old goat, because there were two continuous indentations either side, so that must have been its horns dragging on the ground."

"The goat had come down from the snowy mountains," the third princess said. "I could tell because there were seeds from the alpine flowers in its piles of poop."

"There was rather a lot of poop on the road," the first princess said.

"And a fair amount of wee." The second said.

"Great puddles of it," said the third.

The first said, "That was from the incontinent old lady riding the goat down from the mountain."

The second and third princesses turned to the first, eyebrows raised.

The first said, "I have an incredible sense of smell, it's a blessing and a curse. When I did the orienteering course last year the instructor showed me how to see what animals were in the area by their leavings."

The second asked, "How, exactly?"

The first replied, "You don't want to know."

The third princess said to the dean, "I also think the goat may have been blind in one eye. Because I noticed there was green grass on both sides of the road, but the goat only stopped on one side to graze. Either that or there was too much traffic when the goat had been travelling, so it only ate from one side."

"Very good," the dean said. "You've described our university mascot, Snezhna, exactly. Bit of a worry about the lame leg, we'll have our very best veterinarians assess him."

The princesses were pleased with their observations and their deductions.

The dean said, "I'm sure you're wondering whether you gained admission to this prestigious institution via your brains or your names. The answer is, it's both. You are smart, but you have been born to enormous privilege, which in turn gives you access to the best life has to offer. There are many more people just as smart as you, if not smarter, but they are not here. They have not won life's lottery as you have.

The first asked, "Should we relinquish our places?"

The dean said, "You could do that, and deny yourselves further education. Or, you could work out a better way forward."

The second said, "Oooh, another test!"

The third said, "I know the answer to this one. We'll get our degrees and once we have them, we shall use our wealth to establish education for students across all of Serendy."

The dean smiled and tented his fingers. "Excellent!"

And so that is exactly what the three princesses did.

When Queen Gif heard of their brilliance and their plans for more education across the nation, she couldn't wipe the smile off her face. Her daughters had done the most wonderful thing by using their talents and wealth to benefit other people.

But most of all, it made Gif the most benevolent, generous and clever Queen the island had ever seen, as the princesses named every school they established after their beloved mother.

Wilona's Christmas Ball

BRUGEL'S OWN CINDERELLA

Chapter One

Hanging upside down from the branch of an apple tree early one windy autumn morning, Wilona d'Arella stretched her limbs and reached for a ripe piece of fruit. It filled her hand as she twisted it off its stem, four, five, six times, before coming away with a satisfying *snap*. She tossed the apple, taking into account the wind speed and direction. It landed onto a pile of soft grass. Then it rolled down a gentle, wind-blown slope into a basket; fresh and unbruised, so they could be sold at the market.

"Yes!" She privately cheered for her accurate aim, then carried on plucking apples one by one.

Wilona came from a sprawling farm in the eastern foothills of Brugel, near the northern border with

Styria and Corinthia (whose campaigns for independence continue to this day.)

She lived with her extended family; seven mothers, four fathers and several dozen brothers, sisters, cousins and what-have-yous.

There were thirty-five people living in the family farm. Nobody quite knew exactly who was related to whom, they were just sort of there, living and working and farming, all pulling together. [1]

People who lived in the nearby village of Kronut thought Wilona's farm family were weird. Not that Wilona had time to worry about what others thought of her, she was too busy working.

On this particularly morning, Wilona was picking fruit.

"Wilona!" A voice called out. '*There* you are!"

Parting her long brown blowy hair away from her eyes, Wilona looked about to see who the voice belonged to.

With a twist and a jump, Wilona leapt from the tree and landed on the soft ground below. "Hello Mother Raven, what brings you to the applery today?"

---

1. The nice type of community commune you only find in storybooks. In real world communes, it's much harder work and much less time for leisurely pursuits like picking apples one at a time and aiming them (taking wind direction into account) onto a grassy hill so they fall into a waiting basket.

Mother Raven had long dark hair often tucked up underneath a bonnet as it was now, deep brown eyes and a face full of lines from smiling all her life.

"Mother Hawk has a sore leg, and won't be able to walk to market. I was hoping you might come with me in her place?"

"The Market? How thrilling!" [2] Wilona said.

The Market was where the family took all their produce to sell and swap for the fabrics and food items they couldn't make themselves, like the amazingly sweet pastries the village of Kronut was famous for.

Wilona had never been to Kronut Market, much less spent the day trading. Truth be told, she suddenly felt a little fearful of the prospect of dealing with so many people and trying to sell them things. Would she count the money correctly? Would she suddenly become tongue-tied? Would she be overwhelmed with questions?

But the delight of seeing something new outweighed the fear. She stood up as tall as she could, to appear mature and trustworthy. And brave. Because she didn't want to show how nervous she was.

Her dark hair flickered in the wind and covered her face. Mother Raven tucked the hair away behind her ear and smiled so much her eyes almost vanished under the wrinkles.

---

2. OK, fine, Wilona surely is weird if she thought a day working at the market would be 'thrilling'.

"You're always so helpful Wilona. Stay close to me and don't worry about the crowds."

Wilona picked another few apples to fill the carry basket and asked, "How big are the crowds?"

"It will be something of a crush at times. Lots of people. All talking and moving at once."

"Like milking time?" Because everyone helped with milking and it became noisy and crowded in the milking shed.

"It's even bigger than that. But it's good – the more people who come to market day, the more we sell."

They hitched their goods into the wagon and harnessed the two black steers to pull everything along the road into town. Mother Raven tucked Wilona's hair into a net to keep it neat and tidy. "People tend not to like too much hair on their food, dear."

They walked beside the steers, guiding them, chatting to them, reassuring them of how important and lovely they were. Just your average, normal chatting away to animals, which everyone does.

As Mother Raven had predicted, the market was incredibly noisy and busy, full of traders setting out their wares and loads of visitors milling about. Set up within the walls of the old village keep, the market was protected from the wind, which was a huge blessing, especially as the fish and tripe sellers were down the end of their row. Fish went so much better with lemons than apples anyway.

Keen to learn all she could, Wilona watched as another seller nearby set up her display. The woman placed her green pears in a neat row, turning many of them around so their prettiest side faced out, to hide the dimples and blemishes. Then she removed two items from the display, which looked a little odd.

How clever, Wilona thought, realising what the trader was up to. If a few items were gone already, it looked as if they were already selling! Wilona copied her, removing a few apples from their farm display. Going one better, she took a knife to a not-as-perfect apple and cut it into slices, so that people could sample a taste.

Immediate success! Everyone who had sampled a taste and tasted the sample bought baskets full of apples.

Her apples were glossy and red, so they already looked good. But when people tasted them, they realised how deliciously crunchy and juicy they were.

As the morning wore on, and Wilona refilled the fruit display, she found a little spider sitting on a stem. Carefully she picked the creature up by its silk and placed it back in the basket. Spiders were her friends, especially the orb weavers. They were the best friends a farmer could want. Spiders wove incredible webs that caught all the insects which would otherwise destroy their crops.

Plus the webs looked so beautiful when beaded with morning mist.

Mother Raven traded and haggled with the other farmers and producers, swapping and bartering for the best fillets of fish and cuts of tripe. Meanwhile, Wilona sold their family's produce. They had cheese from their cows, knitted scarves and hats for the oncoming winter, courtesy of their sheep, but the apples were the heroes of their market stall.

So many customers marvelled at how delicious and pretty they were.

"We owe it all to the spiders," Wilona proudly told them.

"Spiders? Oh no, can't stand spiders!" they'd say.

Or worse.

"Spiders? You're *weird*!"

As the afternoon wore on, the same message came through. For some reason, people just couldn't cope with spiders.

Which, to Wilona, was really weird.

As the afternoon wore on, a group of young men entered the market place. They were dressed in fine fabrics and wore jaunty hats with feathers in them. [3]

---

3. Unless this is the very first book you've ever read (in which case, thanks so much for choosing this one!) you'll know a colourful entrance such as this one marks a critical turning point in any fairy tale.

As they approached each trader, the young men made short conversation (Wilona couldn't make out what they were saying) then waved goodbye and moved to the next.

They repeated this with several traders. The traders were always polite and encouraging, but the group didn't purchase a single thing. Although Wilona was young and not well-versed in human behaviour, she'd already seen enough to establish a pattern.

The young men had money – their clothes proved that – but they weren't spending it. It was morbidly fascinating to watch. The traders were being so kind and patient, yet it was for nothing.

Unfortunately, at this very same time Mother Raven hadn't returned from trading with others, so Wilona had to deal with the group on her own as they approached her stall.

The young man in the centre of the group – he seemed to be their leader – strolled towards Wilona's table. Wavy black hair stuck out from beneath his feathered cap. His shirt was open at the neck, with a satiny cravat tucked into it that could indeed be made from real satin. His eyes were hard to discern under the shade of his hat, but they looked brown-ish. She tried not to stare all the same, because ultimately his eye colour didn't really matter, did it?

His mouth had a cheeky tilt as if he enjoyed making jokes. He picked up the largest apple on display and said. "I hear on good authority that yours are the juiciest in town."

His friends thought this was hilarious. They guffawed and laughed as if it was the funniest thing of all time. Talk about an easy crowd.

As the man made to take a bite, Wilona gasped at the sight of a spider crawling out from the apple's base.

"Wait!" she cried, as she reached to swipe it away.

Several horrible misunderstandings happened all at the same time. The man thought Wilona was trying to snatch the fruit away, and pulled the apple even closer toward him.

Wilona lunged to reach for the spider, but lost her balance and toppled over her table of produce.

The young man's friends thought Wilona was trying to attack him, so slapped her arms down and piled themselves over her body.

Apples, limbs and shouts flew everywhere. The men held Wilona so tightly she couldn't speak.

The young man who'd grabbed the apple and started all the trouble suddenly screamed, "Get it off me, get it off me!"

His friends squashed Wilona even more, thinking she was somehow still able to attack despite being buried under three strong lads.

"Spider." Wilona tried to say, but nothing came out.

Mother Raven came rushing back and screamed at the men to unhand her daughter. Just as the weight came away and Wilona could breathe again, she saw her mother do the strangest thing.

Mother Raven had dropped to the ground, her head bowed, and she profusely apologised for the confusion and injury.

"He's not injured!" Wilona croaked out.

"Kneel before your lord and master!" One of the men said.

"The who now?" Wilona asked.

"He's a prince!" Mother Raven said. "Kneel girl. Sharpish!"

Uh oh!

Chapter Two

Wilona dropped to the ground. That satiny cravat the man wore probably was made of real satin after all.

"I'm so sorry, I was only trying to get a spider off the apple. Everything happened at once and I'm so sorry!" She didn't really feel *that* sorry, it's just that she didn't know what else to do and Mother Raven had identified him as a prince.

And also, a prince? Why didn't anyone warn her?

Oh yeah, the fancy the clothes.

And not buying anything – he was probably just visiting and making nice with the traders. That's why everyone was being so kind and patient with him.

Laughing at his jokes. How could she miss all the signs?

As Wilona had spent nearly all her years on the family farm, she'd never seen a prince before, so how was she to know any of this anyway? But still, she should have at least realised something was out of the ordinary.

The prince spat out a chunk of perfectly good, juicy apple. It landed on the ground and became coated in dirt. Then he threw the apple down and the bite mark also developed a dirt crust.

The spider crawled away from the apple. A boot landed hard on top of it, turning it to mush.

"Spiders! Can't stand them." The prince said.

Prince or not, that was no way to behave. Wilona stood up, her face flame-hot from a combination of embarrassment, confusion and recently being crushed by the prince's goon squad.

"You brute!" She yelled before she could stop herself. "What did that spider ever do to you?"

"It could have bitten me."

Wilona said, "No it wouldn't have. You just needed to move it along!"

"Hush, child," Mother Raven said as she stood beside Wilona, to stop her from attacking anyone in her fit of rage. Then she said to the Prince, "It's her first day at The Market, she's very new at this."

The prince adjusted his hat. "You're weird, you know that?"

"And you're cruel to harmless creatures. Do you want to know why these apples are so amazing? Because the spiders are my friends and they catch every single bug in the garden. That's why our fruit is so incredible."

Mother Raven apologised to the prince again and said, "Wilona, please, say sorry and mean it."

But she'd already said sorry. "All right. 'Sorry and mean it'."

"Wilona, please!"

"He started it!"

"My father will hear about this," the prince said.

Wilona had given up wondering what his eye colour was, because by this point she'd gone right off him. "Yeah? Well I've got four of them and they'll hear about you!"

Mother Raven bustled Wilona away, muttering something about checking on the cheeses.

"Who does he think he is anyway?" Wilona complained.

"He's a prince, that's who he is."

"And I suppose that gives him license to be rude and take bites out of food without paying for it, and squash people half to death when all I was trying to do was get the spider off the apple."

Mother Raven sighed. "In some ways my dear, it does."

When the prince returned to Brugel Castle, he handed his horse over to the stable hands, then strolled to the side wing where he had his rooms, so he could dress for family dinner. Family dinners were a weekly formal occasion, and ever since he could remember, it had always been a noisy old time. Because that's what came of having eight siblings all sitting around the one table.

Family dinners were a chance to chat and catch up with everyone.

As tradition dictated, dinner was held before sunset, which became earlier and earlier as the season became colder. Over recent weeks he'd found himself not being very hungry at such an early dinner, then starving later that night. The way to combat such a problem was to load up his plate at the table, eat one or two things, then leave with a full plate he could nibble from later.

Except that today, at the market, he hadn't eaten much, thanks to that apple incident. He'd taken one bite, and despite it being completely delicious, he'd spat it out because of the spider. They really gave him the creeps. Yet now he really craved more apples.

He'd find out where the farm was and pay a visit later.

Reminding him of how little he'd had since breakfast, his stomach groaned and churned with hunger. His mouth began to water at the thought of all the courses he was about to enjoy. Early dinner couldn't come soon enough.

Tradition dictated his father, the Grand Duke of Brugel, sit in the middle of the longest side of the table. His mother, the Grand Duchess, sat opposite. Then the children, who weren't children anymore and honestly were pretty much adults anyway, sat near the parents, according to rank. Nine children. Five sisters sat on the mother's side, eldest closest. Four brothers sat beside their father.

Tradition also dictated nobody speak until their father and mother had spoken, and yet today they were silent.

What had happened to create such unbearable tension? The soup course came and went. Plenty of slurping but no speaking. Then the vegetable course came and went. Same thing. Chomp chomp, but no chatter. Would his father remain mute along with the fruit?

The meats arrived and the servants sliced them - but if the servants noticed the tension, they gave nothing away. Sure as eggs they'd be gossiping in the kitchens.

This quiet tension was definitely not normal. Something was very, very wrong.

Eventually the eldest brother, the Crown Prince,

moved his chair back, stood, bowed to his father and mother and walked out.

He hadn't even touched his sautéed venison.

The rest of the meal was conducted in abject silence, save the chewing of food and sipping of drinks.

The eldest sister, who was the first born of all the siblings, reached her hand out to touch her mother's. The Grand Duchess remained sitting with her back ramrod straight. Well, it was always straight, but today it looked even straighter and ramroddier. With her free hand, she dabbed a napkin at the corner of her mouth.

Something huge was going on, and the young prince really, really wanted in with the gossip.

When the staff arrived to remove their empty plates, he rose and bowed to his parents and made to leave. Any second now his father would question where he was going, demanding he not depart the room until he was dismissed.

His father remained silent.

Something *insanely* huge must have happened. This absolutely was not normal.

Sneaking down the halls, our young hero made his way to The Crown Prince's rooms to see where his brother might be.

Huh? Not there.

The night was dark, but it was still early evening and would be night for many hours yet. CP - his nickname for the Crown Prince, had to be *somewhere*. He found him, eventually, in the stables, brushing down his favourite horse. Not a shining black stallion or magnificent grey, but a steady, plonking great draught horse with fluffy feet, wide head and flared nostrils.

"You took your time," CP said, although he didn't stop brushing.

"Father still hasn't said a word. It's terrible in there. What's going on?"

And another thing, he'd forgotten to take a plate of 'later-ons' which he usually did. Things just weren't going his way at all today.

CP kept brushing the horse for a while, then made a deep sigh. "You'll find out soon enough. Mother and father want me to marry into the Slaegal house and strengthen the alliance."

"And?"

"And?" CP rounded on him. "Have you met them?"

"No. How ugly are they?"

"That's the problem." CP sighed. "It's not that they're ugly. They are all rather handsome and elegant. Yet they are incredibly vapid. I've tried having a conversation with the eldest, but either she's catastrophically shy or, I honestly don't know. I made small talk with the second eldest and she was like a summer castle in winter."

"How's that?"

"Gorgeous to look at but empty inside."

"Oh." Our prince (because we still don't know his name yet, do we? We will soon, just be patient) shrugged and said, "Does that really matter? At least she's pretty."

"Of course it matters! We need to be able to talk to each other."

"Mother and father hardly talk."

CP kept brushing the horse's mane. "And that's exactly why I don't want to end up like them."

"But it's your job to end up like them. And it's not like you don't have a choice at all, you get your pick of the three of them. What's the youngest one like."

CP made a deep sigh which ended up sounding like a groan. "You're not helping. At all."

"Neither are you. Look, we can't help our birth order, and we can't help tradition, but this is hardly a new development. You've known since forever that you have to marry first, and then the rest of us can. The girls can't even start courting until you're wed. Celestine is close to tearing her hair out because you're dragging your feet."

"Celestine is only twenty-three. She'll be fine."

"Not if she doesn't have any hair. Then nobody will have her."

A boot heel crashed into the timber behind them.

CP said, "Speak of the devil, and she appears."

Celestine their elder sister, and the first born of all

the children, but not in line for the throne because of the patriarchy, stepped out of the shadows. "You could think of other people instead of yourself all the time."

"I'm not stopping you from courting. It's mother and father who are demanding I follow tradition."

Celestine clenched her fists. "I'm the laughing stock of Europe because of you!"

CP held his palms out in surrender. "Throw a tantrum with father, not me. He's the one calling the shots." CP fed an apple to the horse, who wrapped his furry lips around it and crunched away, dribbling a little as he did so.

Juicy apples reminded our prince of the young woman at the Kronut market.

Celestine harrumphed regally. "You know I can't marry until after you, so stop blaming everyone else and do your duty. Do you know what they call me? The Old Maid of the East! I should have had three children by now." She grabbed a shovel and scooped up a pile of *something* from a corner. Then she flung the mess in CPs general direction.

Our young prince figured it was high time he left the stables to get away from Celestine's justifiable rage. Plus, he had a real hankering for delicious apples right now.

Chapter Three

As the sun set on the end of the long market day, Wilona and Mother Raven returned to the farm – their wagon loaded with exchanged goods and extra coins.

Mother Raven couldn't wait to tell the family about 'the incident'. Everybody laughed.

Except Wilona.

Embarrassment scorched her face and she fled the house rather than listen to their laughter for one more second. [4]

It was second nature to climb an apple tree and watch the sun setting from the higher branches. An early star shone in the darkening sky. Should she make a wish? This was a fairytale after all. She thought of a good wish, and then a better one came straight after that. After some really good thinking, she came up with the best wish she could imagine:

"I wish that the prince from the market today could appreciate spiders."

She shut her eyes and wished really, *really* hard.

When she opened her eyes, even more stars had come out to play. Her body felt calm and – more importantly – she'd stopped feeling quite so sorry for herself about what an idiot she'd been at the market.

---

4. Very few people truly enjoy being laughed 'at'. Being laughed 'with' is so much better for the ego.

Maybe, as Mother Hawk suggested, she might even be able to laugh at herself when she looked back on this day. Not yet, obviously.

A twig snapped.

"Who's there?" Wilona asked as she looked towards the noise.

"A mere traveller," a male voice said.

It sounded exactly like . . . in the darkness, Wilona's ears did all the work because it was hard to see his face, but he sounded just like the prince from the market.

But what a prince would be doing out here in the dark was anyone's guess.

Plus, he was alone. Where were his overly-pouncy body guards?

"Are you lost?" Maybe it wasn't the prince after all? Maybe she just had prince-on-the-brain?

"Er, no, I am a traveller, and I heard about your apples. I merely came looking to buy some."

At this time of night? "We sold them all at the Kronut Market today."

"Yet your trees are laden with fruit."

Wilona's suspicion rose. "These aren't ripe. If you eat unripe apples, you'll get a stomach ache."

"Yet the apples on the branches near you appear ripe and rosy." He said.

Sure, he wore different clothing to earlier today, and his hat had no feather, but he didn't look like a traveller – moonlight glinted off the shine on his boots

33

for a start. A smile crept over Wilona's face as she said, "If you climb up here, you can have as many apples as you want."

"You want me to climb up th–" He suddenly stopped, as if he'd given himself away.

This confirmed Wilona's suspicions. She climbed down a branch and held her hand out to him. "Here, I'll even help you up."

He looked puzzled for a moment, then he accepted her offer and slapped his hand into hers. It was smooth and soft, the hands of someone who never laboured in the fields.

She hauled him up and he scrambled into a nearby branch, holding on to the trunk to keep his balance. "You can stop acting now, I know who you are," Wilona said.

"What do you mean by that?" He sounded cross. From here, he could take an apple if only he let go of the main trunk and reached out for it. But he didn't seem able to move.

"You've never climbed a tree, and your hands are soft as a kitten's paw. If you're a traveller, then I'm a princess!"

She leaned forward and flicked his silly hat off, exposing his dark hair and confirming his identity. "Good evening, your serene highness."

Clinging to the tree he said, "At least you've learned some manners since this afternoon."

"No wonder you're in a bad mood if you've never

climbed a tree before. Climbing trees is the best thing in the world. What's the point in being a prince if you can't climb a tree when you want to?"

"You will stop making fun at my expense and help me down," he said, ditching any last attempt to sound like a traveller and reverting to his highness-ness.

Wilona knew how awful it was when people made fun of her. Hadn't her family done just the same thing to her? "Sorry. I didn't mean it. I'll grab you some apples to make it up to you."

She climbed up, twisted three of the ripest apples she could reach, tucked them into her shirt and scarpered down again. Once she was level with the prince, she said, "Give me your hand and I'll lower you down."

He held on tightly as she helped him out of the tree and onto firm ground. Then she jumped down beside him and produced the fruit.

Alas, in jumping down, she'd shaken several spiders from a nearby branch. As luck would have it, those very same spiders just happened to land on the prince's hand as he reached for the apples.

"Arrrrgggh!" he yelled as he jumped back in shock. "Horrible things!"

"Stay still!" she ordered him, as she lifted a few stray spiders off his hat. "They really won't bite."

So much for her really, really good wish earlier. The prince hadn't changed one bit. "Why are you so scared of something so small, anyway?"

"Because they're spiders!"

"One more," she reached for his neck and drew the last spider off his collar. "All done."

"These apples better be worth it," he said.

"Of course, they are," she gave him the fruit. "You should reconsider arachnids. They are excellent help in the garden, and they're a wonderful burglar alarm system."

"They are?"

"Yes. Their silk is so strong, that if anyone tries to steal fruit, they walk face-first into webbing. Their screams can be heard right through the valleys."

The prince eyed her with suspicion. "You're not afraid of them at all, are you?"

"They're my helpers."

He wiped the apple to make sure there were no spiders on it, then took a bite. He made a soft groan of delight in the back of his throat.

"I told you they were good."

He chewed for a bit, then said, "You are weird. You're not scared of spiders, and you're not scared of me either."

"Should I be?"

He took another bite and made a slurping noise as the juice sloshed in his mouth. "My whole life, nobody has ever been as rude to me as you."

"I bet your whole life you've never been punished either. You need to earn respect instead of demanding it. If you'd been more respectful at the market, you wouldn't have created such a scene."

"I did not create the scene, you did, when you lunged at me."

"I wouldn't have lunged if you hadn't grabbed the apple before asking."

"I'm a prince, I don't need to ask."

So arrogant! "With that attitude, heaven help us when you become king."

He laughed at that. "We don't have a king, we have a Grand Duke."

"Then I hope you never grow up to be him either!"

He laughed again, "You need a lesson in civics, I'm the youngest of nine children, including four sons. It would take a terrible calamity for me to become Grand Duke."

Chapter Four

Many weeks later, Mother Hawke's leg still hadn't healed enough, and Mother Raven still needed help with Kronut Market. Eventually, as the harvest came to its end and the weather turned colder, and Wilona's promises to behave wore Mother Raven down, she was once again allowed to go to the market.

"I shall treat everyone as if they are royalty," she declared.

Mother Raven sighed. "Just do your best."

This time Wilona was ready for any strange, well-dressed customers who travelled in gangs and chatted to the stallholders without purchasing anything. She even set aside some definitely-spider-free apples on the off-chance the prince and his friends approached their stall.

Alas, no princely visit. Not even some well-dressed ladies, even though the weather proved perfect for thick, fur-lined cloaks and fluffy hats with ear flaps. Wilona loved those hats. They looked stunning when dusted with snow, although it was drizzling rain at this point and the hats looked like drowned ferrets.

A group of men and women wearing the Grand Duke's coat of arms on their hats turned up. *Oooh, excellent.* Wilona was ready to treat them as if they were angels visiting from heaven. Alas (a horrible word which simply makes everything that follows feel like a blow of defeat) the people wearing the Grand Duke's colours didn't talk to the traders. Instead they brushed glue to the wall of the community board and stuck posters to them.

People jostled to read the news.

And the news was definitely jostle-worthy.

The Grand Duke and Grand Duchess of Brugel were hosting a Christmas Ball for their son The Crown Prince. The ball would showcase the Grand Duchy's finest produce to all neighbouring royalty, who were already invited. Traders were encouraged to provide their wares on the night of the ball, in the interest of fostering greater co-operation and trade between the realms.

The Ball itself was not going to be held at Christmas, but in a few weeks' time. If it were actually held at Christmas, everyone would be snowed in and unable to get there, no matter how glorious the snow may look on their furry hats with ear flaps.

"Sounds like a big deal," Wilona said.

Mother Raven nodded her head. "It is a big deal. We shall need to provide the very best apples and cheeses."

"But we've nearly sold all our produce today."

"Then we shall pack up early and take whatever's left home and store them in the cool room, so that we make sure we at least have something to take to the ball.

"Do we get to dance?"

Mother Raven looked thoughtful as she probed her teeth with her tongue, in that thoughtful way women had. "Probably not in the main ballroom, but I'm sure there will be plenty of space for us to dance the night away in the gardens or some such."

A heavy voice boomed out, cutting through the chatter.

"Hear ya'll! Hear ya'll!" It was the town crier, and she was in fine cry today.

"Let it be known that the Grand Duke and Grand Duchess will be hosting a Christmas Ball where all neighbouring royalty will be in attendance."

Wilona was sure she'd just read that. She knew how to read. Her family were clever and they'd taught her. Then again, maybe not everyone could read as well as she? If they did, the town crier would be out of a job.

"Let it be known!" the crier cried out, "That the Grand Duke and the Grand Duchess will also seek to find a bride at the Christmas Ball for the Crown Prince."

That hadn't been on the notice. Wilona wondered why.

Mother Raven said, "Seems a strange way for a bachelor to find a wife; one man and a stack of single women, played out in front of everyone."

"I should probably detest the idea, shouldn't I?" Wilona said. "But I just know I'm going to love it."

Meanwhile at the palace, things were getting even more tense at the weekly family dinners. The alliance between Brugel and Slaegal looked set to unravel because of the Crown Prince's cold feet. Plus, Celestine faced yet another Christmas unwed.

The Grand Duke said, "The ball will go ahead."

The Grand Duchess nodded in agreement, because

that was in her job description. "I agree with the Grand Duke. The ball will go ahead."

CP gave a resigned sigh. "I'm begging you to call it off. Why won't you listen to me?"

"Because it's not about you," the Grand Duke said. "This is about Brugel and Slaegal."

CP looked around the table. "Then get someone else to marry a sister. I'm sure any of my brothers would jump at the chance."

The Grand Duke scowled.

The Grand Duchess said, "The reason your brothers cannot choose a sister is because they will not one day be Grand Duke, whereas you will."

"What if I refuse?"

Nobody answered, and for a while at the table, the silence was exquisitely excruciating, until the Grand Duke said to his wife, "You've been doing marvellously with preparations. I've never seen the ballroom look so fine."

The Grand Duchess may have been answering her husband, but she looked pointedly at her eldest son and said, "Thank you, Your Grace. It's an honour to serve."

"I give up," CP said, throwing his hands in the air, "I can't put up with this relentless pressure. I'll choose a bride at the ball. Are you happy now?"

The Grand Duchess beamed with delight.

The Grand Duke nodded to CP. "Do your duty."

CP gave a resigned sigh.

The next-born son clapped his hands together and said, "I'm so glad that's sorted. Now on to more important things. There's a fruit tree I'm keen to import, and I'm sure it will grow well in some of the warmer, more protected areas of Brugel. It's called a peach tree. The fruit is small and furry, and the pressed juice is apparently even more delicious than grapes.

"Is it now?" The Grand Duke said. "That certainly sounds interesting."

Chapter Five

The d'Arella family spent the next few weeks in a flurry of activity. The mothers gathered the very pick of the harvest and stored it in the cold cellars under layers of hessian to stop them from spoiling. The fathers measured everyone and sewed new clothing for them to wear to the ball. Nobody was under any illusion they would be attending the really royal part of proceedings inside the ballroom – that would be for visiting dignitaries and royals – but if they were well-dressed enough and presented beautiful food, they were sure they'd be allowed to watch.

The night of the ball came. Wilona and her sisters and brothers and mothers and fathers and cousins and what-have-yous each walked with a small cart or barrow laden with the very best produce. As they walked, Wilona and her sisters traipsed through the fields, gathering spider silk onto their dresses, making them shine in the moonlight.

By the time they arrived at the palace, their gowns were glistening and luminous. Wilona took the extra step of walking close to the low branches, adding sparkly fresh spider silk to her hair.

Other farmers had gone to great lengths to show off their produce, decorating their wagons and carts with puppets and animla cutouts. Others had fruit and vegetable themes. There was even a carriage decorated to look like an enormous pumpkin, a fruit from the new worlds that had recently become popular.

Wilona and her family gathered near the palace entry gates, watching the parade of royals from neigbouring principalities, duchies and grand duchies arrive. Their clothing glistened as they climbed out of their carriages – but not because of spider webs. They had real jewels sewn into the fabric of their clothes!

Once all the visiting dignitaries were inside the castle, the staff opened the gates so the farmers could set up their displays in the gardens.

Sneaking away from her family, Wilona jogged up the castle steps to catch a glimpse of the ball through the enormous windows.

There was the Grand Duke and the Grand Duchess, wearing the finest clothes Wilona had ever seen. The town crier – using her less deafening inside voice – announced the arrival of each guest.

The Crown Prince – well, who else could it be – stood there and smiled and shook everyone's hand, then triple-kissed their cheeks to welcome them.

Nearby, someone out on the landing cleared their throat. Wilona looked up to see the throat-clearer was the young prince.

He smiled and asked, "Pray tell, why are you not inside dancing?"

"Oh! You startled me." Remembering her manners (a rare thing) she made a short curtsey and explained. "I don't belong in there."

"But you must be a visiting Princess or daughter of someone important. At the very least a Lady of some established family?"

"You're teasing me, My Lord. It's good to see you again since you last visited the applery."

His jaw dropped open as he recognised her. "You're the girl who loves spiders!"

"The one and only. Wilona d'Arella." This time she made a more elegant curtsey, her silk-covered skirts sparkling as she did so. "And I know you're the youngest son, but you have me at a disadvantage, as I still do not know your name."

"How very informal of you to ask. But since you have, it's Iosef."

"I'm pleased to meet you, My Lord Iosef." For some reason, Wilona found herself grinning. Overcome with self-consciousness, she curtseyed again.

Had he really not recognised her or was he merely flirting? It was so hard to tell.

The music from the ballroom inside struck up, the familiar tune so rich it permeated the walls and filled the front garden. People in the forecourt stopped setting up their wares for a moment and began to dance.

Iosef smiled at Wilona and bowed politely, extending his hand. "My lady, may I have this dance."

A giggle slipped out as Wilona took his hand. "Why certainly, My Lord."

They danced and twirled and kept time with the beat. Naturally he'd had dancing lessons and stepped lightly around her. Not having had the same advantages, Wilona was not as light on her feet, but the music filled her with confidence and sure footing. Plus, Iosef proved such a natural leader she easily followed the steps.

The atmosphere became intoxicating as everyone outside in the garden danced with as much spirit as those inside. Perhaps even more so, not being restricted to expectations of behaviour and decorum.

Every now and then when the music stopped, and Wilona caught her breath, she had a peek inside at all the proper-people. They weren't smiling as much. If anything, they looked a little concerned.

The only people smiling were the crown prince and the woman he danced with.

"He's still dancing with the same lady," Wilona

said. "I thought he was supposed to dance with everyone and then choose a bride?"

"That was the plan," Iosef said, an endearing furrow of concern forming at the top of his nose. "He did promise our parents he would choose a bride."

"Unless my eyes deceive me, he does appear to have chosen one. Who is she?" Wilona asked.

Iosef made that furrow again. "I don't know. She is not wearing any house colours that I recognise."

"Well, your brother certainly seems to have made up his mind about her. He's not even looking at anyone else."

"Oh dear."

"Why is that bad? I thought the whole point of The Christmas Ball was so he could choose his wife?"

"He was supposed to choose one of the sisters from the House of Slaegal. To make an alliance between Slaegal and Brugel."

"What about your other brothers, can't they make the alliance instead?"

While Wilona and Iosef had been dancing, her body had warmed, but now a chill settled into her neck. Gentle snow began to fall, casting the palace grounds in a fairytale picture-perfect atmosphere. And yet something was very wrong in the ballroom.

Iosef said, "Second sons aren't worth as much."

"I guess that's why you can sneak out here and not be missed."

"I don't sneak."

Wilona smiled broadly. "My deepest apologies, My Lord. All the same, you didn't deny you wouldn't be missed."

"This is my eldest brother's event, not mine. In the grand scheme of things, I will be little more than a footnote in history."

The music struck up again. In the gardens, the farmers and producers returned to setting up their displays, but they swayed to the music and tapped their feet as they worked.

Wilona turned to Iosef and made a curtsey. "I've had a lovely time. Thank you so much for the honour. But . . . perhaps you need to get back inside and dance with the other ladies, so they don't feel left out."

"That would be the sensible thing to do," he said. Although he didn't move.

Wilona smiled. "Something tells me you think being sensible is overrated?"

He smiled again and held his hand out to take Wilona's. "You would be correct. I'd much rather stay here with you. However, it *would* be prudent if I returned to assist my family in this most delicate matter of my eldest brother casting his heart in the wrong direction."

Wilona curtseyed again, because her brain had gone blank and she couldn't think of anything else to say.

Then he kissed the back of her hand in farewell

and her body heated so much it virtually melted the snow off her shoulders.

Iosef went back inside and Wilona watched and waited until she could see him re-enter the ballroom. OK, now he was safely back inside, she should get back to helping her family, but something caught her eye. A group of people inside the ballroom were huddled together near a doorway. Then some of them slipped out. Rushing towards the bannister, Wilona leaned over to see seven or eight men and women mount waiting horses. As they flicked their cloaks back, she saw the lining underneath.

Decorated with the flag of Slaegal.

This definitely looked like something she should tell her family about, so she dashed down the stairs and soon found them.

"To the fields," Mother Raven said. "We need more spider silk."

They raced off in their cloaks and made their way to the open fields, where spider silk draped between spears of winter wheat grass. Wilona draped her cloak across the grass, covering the fabric in layers and layers of strong spider silk.

Satisfied at the thick coating, she and the rest of her family returned to the palace grounds.

By now it was getting very late. Wilona checked through the windows to see what was happening inside. The music was still playing, and the people inside were still dancing. The crown prince remained dancing with the same woman, who looked utterly lovely and danced divinely. It was painfully obvious that no other lady would get a look-in.

The clocks chimed. Midnight already?

Something very strange happened in the ballroom. The woman dancing with the crown prince pulled back, her hand over her mouth in shock.

Then something *really* strange happened.

She ran off.

Why would she do such a thing when she clearly had him all to herself in a crowded ballroom? Had the prince said something wrong?

Uh-oh, the lady was running towards the balcony exit!

Wilona hid behind a Brugelian column to keep watching events as they unfolded.

The lady cast a longing look back at the ballroom she'd escaped, then she turned and fled down the steps.

A few heartbeats later, the Crown Prince followed. He called out, "Wait! I don't even know your name!"

Idiot, Wilona thought. *They'd had so much time together and he hadn't asked that?*

The lady had fled, through the front garden, past the traders in their spider silk lined cloaks and out the front gates. As far as Wilona knew, she'd kept right on running.

The prince made it a few steps down, then stopped to pick something up.

By now, everyone was looking at the prince, so it

made no sense for Wilona to remain hidden. She stepped out to see the crown prince holding an ornate shoe that the lady had lost on the stairs on the way down.

"I must find her," the prince said as he saw Wilona approach.

"That should be easy. She's left pretty distinctive footsteps behind her."

Indeed the fresh footsteps in the newly fallen snow would be simple to follow, as they had one shoe print and one bare footprint leading directly out the front gates and away towards the village.

The crown prince rushed off to follow.

The moment the prince vanished, the traders started chatting about what was going on. Wilona didn't have time to join in, as at that moment she saw a panic-stricken Iosef on the top of the stairs.

Wilona rushed to his side. In doing so, she saw and heard the commotion from inside, as the ballroom doors were now wide open.

Wilona said, "She ran off, dropped a shoe, your brother picked it up and then ran after her. As long as the snow doesn't fall too thickly, they should be pretty easy to follow."

"Thank you. I'll send his personal guard to follow."

Which he did.

When Iosef returned, Wilona remembered the other drama from a little earlier. "Something else happened while you were in there. A group from Slaegal rode away. I don't know where to."

"Wait, what?"

Wilona repeated herself.

Iosef turned pale. "They probably rode back to Slaegal. No doubt returning with reinforcements. But I've just sent our guards away, to chase my brother. The palace is defenceless."

"We've thought about that. My family and the traders have already coated outselves in spider silk on the off chance–"

The sound of thundering horse hooves filled their ears.

"Shut the gates!" Iosef cried out.

The traders and staff below worked hard to bring the gates together to lock them, but the snow drift and cold made it a difficult exercise.

Suddenly arrows flew through the air!

"Get down!" Wilona yelled, throwing her cloaked arm out to protect Iosef.

People ran screaming back into the ballroom for safety.

Iosef either didn't hear, or was too slow as another arrow flew close to them. It hit Wilona in the forearm. She howled in pain. Arrows really hurt!

But it hadn't pierced.

Iosef's face beamed in surprise as he examined Wilona's spider-silk covered arm. The arrow had bounced off.

"What sorcery is this? You are unharmed."

"It's not sorcery, it's spider silk. And I'm going to have a massive bruise there tomorrow."

"Come with me, we must cover the remaining guards in spider silk." Iosef and Wilona crawled away, back into the ballroom, where they found people cowering in fear at the sudden invasion.

They collected a few dozen fighters and raced out another door, all of them following Iosef, who was following Wilona, to the farming fields where they could cover themselves with protective silk.

Mother Wren, despite her bad leg, was still in the field, coating scarves and hats with spider silk, turning them into make-do gorgets and helmets.

As soon as everyone was properly protected, it was time to get back and 'storm the castle', which, from their point of view, was defending it.

The invader's arrows bounced off their newly protective clothing, but they still made a walloping impact that rattled Wilona's bones. Until now, Wilona had thought herself reasonably fit. After all, she climbed trees and worked long days. But she wasn't battle-fit. Not by any stretch.

Thankfully, Iosef was battle-fit. He borrowed Wilona's spider-silk covered cloak and charged at the enemy. In a few moves he ripped a bow out of their hands and used it to jab and stab at them. The rest of the traders followed his lead and rounded on the invaders, overwhelming them with sheer numbers –

and weaponised fruit and vegetables, which they threw at their heads.

Somebody called out, "Load the unsold tripe into the trebuchet!" A second later, the sky filled with offal and landed hard on the enemy.

Outnumbered and outsmarted, the attackers fled.

A rousing cheer erupted in the gardens. Their displays and carefully arranged produce were scattered all over the ground, but they'd won.

The Grand Duke and Grand Duchess stepped out from the ballroom and cheered the result, realising what a close-run thing it had been.

Iosef rushed back to Wilona's side and returned her cape, now splashed with myriad colours from the chunks of fruit and vegetables that had rained down on the enemy. "Thank you for the incredible, life-saving fabric. I felt invincible under this . . . well, it was nothing short of a dreamcoat."

Wilona's face hurt from smiling so much.

Iosef added, "Your quick thinking and clever family has truly saved Brugel tonight."

"You're very welcome," Wilona gushed.

Iosef suddenly appeared nervous. "I realise we don't know each other very well, and it could simply be the rush of adrenaline from defeating an invading enemy, but can we start kissing now?"

"Oh yes!"

And so they did, their lips met in a rush of relief and excitement, not much panache but loads of passion as they knocked teeth on lips in their eagerness. Soon they found a better rhythm and style; she placed her hand on the nape of his neck, he wrapped his arms around her waist and pressed her into his body. Their breaths came out in little puffs of steam, which was all rather lovely, as the snow gently fell about them, dusting their shoulders and heads in magic.

"You're excellent at this," Iosef said.

"I'm a quick learner," Wilona said.

As they kissed a little more, he raised his hand to her face and tucked a lock of hair behind her ear. A spider crawled out of her hair. He flinched.

Wilona said, "Oops, sorry about that."

"You know what? I need to get over my silly fears. Especially as these tiny creatures saved the castle tonight."

"They're not all tiny," Wilona rubbed her nose against Iosef's in tender affection. "You should see the orb weavers. Big as a side plate."

"Don't push it," he said, but he kept smiling. "Baby steps, please."

"Of course." She pressed her lips agains his again, her whole body warming at the contact.

This kissing thing. It was sensational!

A few hours later, as people cleaned up the mess and

tended to the injured after the battle, the Grand Duke and Duchess declared a national holiday the next day, to spread the word of the incredible events that had happened.

Wilona and Iosef had helped a little with the clean up, but they also kept sneaking off and kissing when they thought nobody was looking, because they'd discovered they really liked kissing each other.

The Crown Prince returned to the palace with his runaway dance partner, who by now had both her shoes.

The Grand Duke said, "You've put the enitre Brugel and Slaegal alliance at risk. But it's still fixable if you agree to marry one of the Slaegal sisters."

CP shook his head. "No father. I've made up my mind. Svedeta and I will marry. There's nothing you can do to change my mind."

"Maybe she'll change her mind when you're penniless and homeless," the Grand Duke said.

"We've already discussed it. I'm abdicating my inheritance. One of my brothers can do their duty. I'm out. We're going to live in the mountains and raise snowgoats."

Thunder filled the Grand Duke's face. "Wife! Fetch me another son, this one's defective."

The Grand Duchess spoke up and said, "No dear, I think you mean he's *defecting*. Do take care Wilberick, I shall miss you terribly. And you my dear, Svedeta is it? Please take care of my darling boy. And let me know if there's anything I can do for you."

Svedeta made a curtesy, "Thank you, Your Grace, I appreciate that."

Standing a little way back, still wrapped in Iosef's embrace, Wilona watched the events unfold. "Wow, so he didn't pick one of the Slaegal sisters. I wonder what will happen now?"

The moment Wilona said those prophetic words, the next eldest son appeared at the Grand Duke's side.

"Olfrick, get your staff to fill a carriage with the best produce you can find, then get in it and offer yourself to whichever Slaegal sister will have you. We will have this alliance if it's the last thing we do!"

Wilona whispered to Iosef, "He seems really, really angry."

Iosef took Wilona by the hand and stepped away as quietly as he could, not wanting his father to see them. Alas, as luck, fate and the plot would have it, he stepped on a snail, making a loud crack as the shell broke beneath his foot.

"What are you doing?" His father cried out. "A spy in the nest?"

"It's only me, your youngest son," Iosef said, as if to remind his father not to chop his head off. "I found the person responsible for saving us all. This brave woman had the quick thinking to cover our cloaks in spider silk, making them impenetrable to attack. They fired their cross bows and threw spears, and we came away bruised but not bleeding. All thanks to Wilona."

It took a while to explain everything that had happened. It also took a lot of fast talking to calm the Grand Duke down from his high dudgeon. He'd just seen an alliance fall through, his eldest son completely disobey him and then throw over his responsibilities to his country to raise livestock.

"Prove it," The Grand Duke said.

Iosef took the cloak from Wilona and placed it over his elbow. "Stab me in the arm."

"I could stab you in the stomach, you've left yourself wide open."

"This is just a demonstration, father."

"All right then." He took the ceremonial blade out of his hip holster and made for his son's limb. "Stab stab." He pushed it into the fabric.

Iosef exposed his skin. It was marked, but unbroken, just as he'd promised.

"Father, we may be enemies now with Slaegal, but they won't get the better of us if your armies are protected with spider silk."

The Grand Duke looked at the cloak. "Spiders, you say?"

"I know, right?"

"Can't say I'm a huge fan. They give me the creeps."

Iosef laughed. "Same here. But recently, I've learned to appreciate them."

Wilona smiled and hugged Iosef, realising that after all this craziness, the wish she'd made that night in the applery really had come true.

Chapter Six

In the weeks to come, The Grand Duke and Duchess made Iosef an Earl and gifted him an advisory position with the Brugelish army. The spider silk made the most excellent armour. Lightweight, easy to obtain and most importantly, it didn't rust. Every night soldiers walked to the meadows and draped their cloaks over the spider silk, and the next night, the spiders built their webs again.

They alternated meadows so that the spiders wouldn't get too exhausted, making webs only to lose them completely, and not be able to catch any food. It was still vitally important the spiders carry out their first responsibility of eating as many other insects as possible, in order to protect the crops.

The crops themselves grew more beautiful as farmers across the land understood how useful a field full of spiders could be. The plentiful spiders attracted hungry birds, who ate the spiders instead of the grains, another magnificent benefit.

To recognise how vital spiders were, The Grand Duke and Grand Duchess added a six-pointed spider web to the Brugelish coat of arms. The spider web was their secret armour, hiding in plain sight.

The people of Brugel became so enamoured of spiders and their silk, they worshipped the hexagonal shape. Over time, as the history books show, this love of the spider web shape became the basis of their national flag. To this day Brugel still has the only hexagonal flag in the world.

Crown Prince Wilberick was no longer the crown prince. He lived with his lovely bride Svedeta in the mountains. They raised champion snow goats who won so many competitions the organisers had to create special categories just to make sure others had a chance of winning. Introducing new rules to snowgoating competitions proved difficult, as nobody could find the original set of rules, including that all entrants in snowgoating had to be actual goats, not sheep or pigs wearing anoraks. But that is a thrilling and charming story for another time.

But the most important thing that happened, obviously, was between Wilona and Iosef. Iosef learned how to climb trees (which also helped with military strategies, for spotting advancing troops.) Their apples and produce continued to be incredibly delicious and bountiful as well.

He proposed to Wilona, who said yes, and they lived happily ever after …

… Oh OK, here's the scene in full. Because you

really want to see this one play out properly for full satisfaction. Can't blame you for that.

They were in the applery with the promise of spring in the air, but there were no apples as it was completely the wrong time of year for that. Wilona and Iosef were up in the tree, and sure enough, they were k-i-s-s-i-n-g.

Iosef said to Wilona, "You're a natural at this."

Wilona smiled. "What exactly am I a natural at? Pruning apple trees or kissing?"

Iosef said, "Definitely both, but the kissing is so much more enjoyable, and far less work."

"I noticed that." Wilona kissed Iosef again, then said, "But the pruning ensures a bountiful harvest in autumn."

Iosef grinned rather wickedly and said, "I'm sure there's some kind of double entendre with the whole *bountiful harvest* thing, but I can only think of one thing."

They giggled and spent the rest of the afternoon kissing, between pruning sessions. Wilona was light on her feet in the trees, and incredibly agile with the hand saw as she trimmed away branches to open up the centre of the tree. Iosef gathered the pruned branches off the ground and piled them into neat stacks. His hands were not as buttery soft as they'd once been, which delighted him.

A spider crawled off a branch and onto his hand. He yelped - it was still an automatic reflex - but then he laughed at himself. "Off you go little fella," he said as he flicked his hand towards the wood pile, so the spider could fall gracefully down an invisible yet incredibly strong silk cord. The wonderful silk that had saved Brugel at the Christmas Ball.

"Is everything all right?" Wilona asked. "I heard you yelp."

"Oh yes. Everything is wonderful," Iosef said. "Look at this, I have a callus on my hand from working!"

"I have stacks of them," Wilona climbed out of the tree and held her palms up to brag.

Iosef took her hands in his. "You've made me so happy. And your quick thinking and your love of spiders saved the country."

Then Iosef dropped to both knees, as was the Brugelish custom. Dropping to both knees made it much harder for the man to get back to his feet and give chase, should his intended bride not want anything to do with him and flee.

"Oooooh, I know where this is going, you're about to..."

"Can I get the words out?"

"No! I mean Yes!"

"But I haven't asked you."

"Hurry up and ask me."

He truly was trying. "Wilona d'Arella will you do …"

"Yes"

"… Me the honour?"

"I said yes."

"Of being my military advisor."

"Yes yes – what??? Hang on, what did you say?"

He knelt there, looking up into her eyes as a wicked grin spread over his face. "Just kidding. Marry me."

"You bet!"

She helped him back onto his feet and they hugged and kissed for a while, getting absolutely no work done at all.

After a fairly decent session of kissing and cuddling, Iosef spoiled the mood. "There is a slight problem though. As the youngest, I have to wait until the others are married before I'm allowed to."

"That's a stupid rule."

"Tell me about it."

"Would they even notice if you married anyway?" Wilona asked. "I don't think my parents would notice – there are so many of us here, one more or less wouldn't matter."

"You're so clever." Iosef said, thoroughly kissing her again.

In the months to come, Wilona and Iosef secretly married. In the years to come, their children were easily absorbed into the bustling numbers at the family farm, so The Grand Duke and Duchess were none the wiser.

The next eldest son of the Grand Duke and Duchess ended up obeying his parents and did marry one of the Slaegal Sisters. The trouble was, Slaegal's royal family took this as an insult anyway, and relations between the two countries remained tense. Around this time The New Crown Prince began importing peach trees into Brugel. The fruit crop wasn't as robust as he'd hoped, so he stored them in enormous terracotta urns where they fermented and, to everyone's delight, created a rather tasty liquor that became incredibly popular.

Eventually, after Wilona and Iosef had been together for six years and already had four children, the Grand Duke announced that they had his permission to marry. Which they did, in winter, wearing thick coats that hid how close Wilona was to having her fifth child.

The wedding cake was decorated with spider webs, both real and frosted. They were hoping to start a trend, but it never really caught on.

And they all lived merrily and messily ever after.

Special Thanks to the Tripe Marketing Board UK

The author would like to thank the Tripe Marketing Board, UK, for assistance in researching the little-known links between Brugel and tripe. For information and career opportunities:

https://tripemarketingboard.co.uk/jobs.php

Customer Service Advisors

Do you like tripe? Do you dislike people?

If you can answer yes honestly to both these questions then you may have what it takes to become a Tripe Advisor customer service advisor.

Tripe Advisor is the UK's no 1 tripe advisory service. It is a wholly owned subsidiary of the Tripe Marketing Board and our Freephone service takes dozens of calls every year. We are now looking to recruit customer service advisors.

As a Tripe Advisor customer service advisor, you will be answering questions such as:

Where can I buy tripe?
What is the safest way to   dispose of unwanted tripe?
Is tripe safe to eat?
Does tripe taste as disgusting as it looks?
Help, I have just accidentally eaten some tripe. What should I do?
I have just eaten some tripe and am perspiring heavily. Is this normal?
Where can I buy vegetarian tripe?
Is tripe safe for babies?
Is tripe safe for dogs?
Is tripe safe?

We currently have vacancies in our Mumbai, Darjeeling, Kuala Lumpur and Preston call centres. You will receive a competitive salary and as much free tripe as you can eat.

Ref: TMBCA

The Monster

Once upon a time there was a village by a lake with a monster problem. Families lived in fear that their children would be taken in the night by the terrible and strange beast.

Not that anyone had ever seen the monster. Not with any real clarity. Some claimed they had. One described it as three metres tall with glowing red eyes. Another said it had six arms, and teeth like the fangs of a sabre-cat. Somebody else claimed the monster was made of pure shadow and sin, and could inhabit the shape of a hedgehog and hide in the forest.

This was horribly unfair to hedgehogs and led to many people hunting them on the off chance they were monsters in disguise. This is because the towns-people were stressed, their children were being taken by something horrible out there, and they were lashing out.

After the fifth child vanished in the space of a few months, the townspeople demanded something be done about the brute roaming around and stealing their children.

The town alders held an enormous meeting. Everyone in the village attended. It became pretty heated. People started yelling and screaming. Groups of parents decided they'd patrol the village at night and make sure the monster couldn't get in. That seemed to be a pretty good solution. It calmed people down to think there was something practical they could do. So they started a roster and parents signed on to various shifts. Night after night they patrolled the outskirts of the village, making sure no monsters could get in.

But somehow the monster got in anyway, and stole a child right out from under their chins.

The townspeople gathered once more and demanded even bigger patrols. Every single villager over the age of sixteen was rostered to join the patrols.

The children were ordered to sleep in the safety of the alderhaus, a big hall where the alders and the mayor met to discuss important issues.

This was seen as a pretty good deal for the children, who treated the entire episode like a continuous series of slumber parties.

The children weren't sleeping at night because they were having too much fun. And the parents, having patrolled the village all night, were exhausted.

Everybody was getting really tired and cranky, which was hardly surprising.

Then another child vanished and people were so tired, upset and fearful, they were just about ready to burn the entire village to the ground in frustration.

Everyone gathered for another meeting and people shouted even louder than before. When people had shouted so much their voices began to wear out, a young woman stood up and made an astonishing speech. Her voice shook as she spoke.

"I know who the monster is. It's the mayor. He's in a position of trust in the community and has taken advantage of our fears and obedience to help himself to the children."

The people were stunned into silence.

The mayor stared at the woman and said, "That's a disgusting lie! How dare you! Has our village not suffered enough that you turn us against each other?"

"But it's true! I saw you! I've been keeping an eye on you. *You're* the monster!"

The villagers screamed the alderhaus down in their outrage that one of their own would point the finger at such an esteemed member of the community.

"She's a witch!" One of the alders called out. "She's the one who's been taking the children!"

This accusation satisfied the villagers, who were tired and fearful of everything, so weren't in a very good frame of mind to conduct self-examination.

The woman, seeing the villagers' anger, tried to flee.

"She's running away because she's guilty!" someone claimed.

The villagers set upon the woman and dragged her to the lake, where they dunked her in the water. She spluttered and cried out for help, but nobody stepped forward to help her, because nobody knew how to stop the burning anger consuming them. The dunking continued until they were all quite satisfied that the witch was dead.

After the dunking, things settled down a lot more. The patrols stopped – because they were exhausted and needed sleep. The children returned to their homes and everyone started getting proper sleep again.

And no children vanished for such a long time, the entire incident was hardly ever mentioned again. People were happy to believe the children were safe now that the witch was dead.

But still, the fear niggled at them. If a witch had managed to ingratiate herself into the village, how could they stop that happening again?

Instead of patrolling the outskirts of the village, the alders patrolled inside the village, introducing extra rules to make it very clear that witches were not welcome, and anyone displaying witch-like behaviour would be asked to leave. And by 'asked to leave' they meant dunked in the lake until they were dead.

Turns out, the village really did have a huge monster problem, but it was all too hard to admit the monster was a respected member of the community, so they took the easy path and blamed women.

The Town With No Children

A TALE OF WOE TO CURDLE YOUR HEART
FASTER THAN LEMON JUICE IN MILK.

Back in the old days, people did not travel much beyond their own village borders. This is because there were no cars or trains, and the only way to travel far was to walk or ride a horse. Either way, it was hard to travel more than thirty lachters a day. (An old measurement, where five jows made one buddam, and seven buddams made one lachter, which is about a kilometre in today's language, give or take a girah or two.)

People lived in the one village all their lives, and knew everyone else as well. In this one village, called Ammelinn, the people were prospering. The fields produced a bumper crop of wheat, carrots, turnips and hops, which meant plenty of beer, soup and bread for everyone.

When they harvested the crops, they had so much produce the storage bins overflowed. People tied up the excess in cloth bags and stored them anywhere they could. In cellars, under beds and even in the roof space. When they were full, the people stored them in the children's desks at the school. The children enjoyed snacking on the carrots during lessons.

It would have been smart to construct more secure grain stores, but nobody thought of that. This is what happens when people live in the one village for generations – you don't visit new places and get fresh ideas, nor do you get new people bringing their ideas in with them.

The excess food attracted rats. And the rats were really, really happy about that. They ate the wheat in the rooftops, they ate the turnips in the cellars and they ate the hops under the beds. People tried to shoo them away, but the rats were living in the wall and roof cavities, and breeding at a terrifying rate.

Then the rats charged into the school. The children screamed and tried to chase the rats away with broomsticks and books and even the slates they wrote on. The rats lunged for the carrots hidden in the desks, and bit the children when they tried to pick them off and throw them out.

The children returned home covered in rat bites. Their parents had no idea what to do. This had never happened before.

The children became sicker and sicker from the rat bites, which festered and oozed. The school was deserted as all the kiddies were home sick.

That's when the stranger came to town, and that's when things became seriously weird and pretty horrible.

The strange woman was dressed in layers of colourful clothing and had musical instruments with her. She said to the mayor, "I have removed rats from other villages, and I can get rid of the rats here as well, for a fee."

The mayor looked at her and asked, "How do I know you're any good?"

The stranger produced a letter from the mayor of another village, which said how delighted they were that the stranger had rid their village of rats. What was even more delightful was the recovery of the village's children, who were no longer oozing pus.

The mayor was suspicious. "How do I know you weren't responsible for sending all the rats from that village to ours?"

The stranger said, "There are many villages in these parts who are suffering rat infestations. The bumper crops have provided all the food the rats will ever need, and so they are breeding like … well, like rats really. If you're not interested, I can move on to the next village."

The mayor said, "Show us how you get rid of the rats first, then we'll think about making it official."

The stranger said, "You want me to work for you, for free?"

The mayor said, "We don't know whether you're

any good, so it stands to reason we should see whether or not this will work. After all, what's the point of paying you, if you don't actually get rid of the rats?"

This went on for quite some time. And by quite some time, we're talking days of negotiations, rates of pay, key performance indicators, the works. All the while the rat numbers kept increasing, because times were very good for them, while the children got sicker and sicker.

Spots turned to pox. Pox turned to pukes. Pukes turned to rivers of ... urgh!

The stranger was also getting cross by this point, and a little sick herself. "Do you want me to get rid of the rats or not? Nobody is giving me a spare room, so I'm sleeping out here under the stars, dying of exposure."

"Fine," the mayor relented. "I'll give you some of the money now, and the rest when the rats are gone."

The stranger set about catching the rats. She played an incredible tune on her flute, which mesmerised many of the rats. While they were half stupefied, the stranger grabbed her hooks and snares and bags and traps. She moved like a whirlwind, snagging and bashing those rats, like a rodent-catching machine. All while that beautiful, tantalising music played on.

She bagged every single female rat.

She went to the mayor and asked for the rest of her payment. "The rats cannot breed any more. The females are all gone, the males will soon die out."

The mayor quibbled. "The job is only half done! In the mean-time, we need to make bread and beer and sell them to our neighbouring villagers to earn money, and we don't have any traders coming right now. They seem to be staying away because of the plague the children have come down with. And anyway, there are still male rats around and they're getting aggressive."

The stranger sighed deeply. She knew it would come to this. "Your excuses will not put food on my table or buy me new clothes, which the rats have pretty much destroyed. Pay me in gold."

More haggling ensued. The mayor offered to write her a letter to praise her rat catching skills, which she could take to the next town, and earn more money there.

The stranger lost patience. "Mayor, I've had enough. If you don't pay me the rest of my fee, I will curse this town so that nobody in the village ever has a girl child again. You'll be cursed with boys who will be forced to travel away to seek new lives, which will deplete the village. Mark my words, no girl child will ever be born in this village again."

"I'd like to see you try," the mayor said. No sooner had he said those fateful words than the stranger played her tune again.

This time, instead of rats, every pregnant woman

in the village walked towards the mayor's house, hypnotised by the beautiful, entrancing music.

"This is your last chance, mayor, pay me or suffer the consequences."

"You're bluffing."

And so the stranger played her tune and the women spontaneously went into labour, which was not only incredibly dramatic, but messy as well.

The villagers came running with fresh towels and sheets and set to boiling their sharpest knives in water. One after another baby screamed into the world. Every one of them male.

The stranger turned to the Mayor. "I warned you."

The stranger left town, and within a few years, it became obvious to everyone in the village of Ammelinn that none of the expectant mothers would give birth to girls. Everyone had boys. And a few years after that, they realised that without girls, the town's population would wither and die. Younger families left the town, knowing there would be no future for their sons. Ammelinn became known as the town with no children. The story was twisted and changed to blame the stranger for stealing the children with her music, but we know the truth.

The moral of the story:

Some people claim the moral of the story is to beware of strangers. This is of course one interpretation, made by people who don't get out much.

Another interpretation is that workers should never give their labour for free if everyone else is gaining a benefit except them.

But the real moral of the story is: don't screw over your children's futures for the sake of saving a few dollars today.

Jacqueline and the Magic Beans

*How the magic of coffee came to Brugel
and people got things done!*

Chapter One

Many generations ago, in a small corner of Brugel, lived a poor, poor woman called Grunhilda, and her daughter Jacqueline. They were so poor, they had sold all their furniture and nearly all their clothes. They'd also started selling off their roof tiles, just so they could get a loaf of bread to eat.

Her husband, Grunbillda had signed up years earlier to join the war. He wasn't particularly fussy about which war, just as long as whichever army he joined offered two hot meals a day and a uniform to keep him warm and a tent over his head to keep him dry.

Grunhilda and Jacqueline had barely made it through another gruelling winter when Grunhilda had become so weak from sleeping on the floor (she'd sold her bed) and standing up to eat (they'd also sold their dining table) that she looked around and wondered what they possibly had left to sell.

Jacqueline, the daughter, turned to her mother and said, "Dearest mother, we have nothing left but these four walls, half a roof and our snowgoat. Whatever shall we do?"

The mother looked at her and said with a sigh, "Fye! If only it wasn't illegal to eat your children."

Jaqueline said, "I beg your pardon?"

Grunhilda said, "Sorry, what? No, I meant, take the snowgoat to market and sell him for the best price you can get."

Jacqueline took their snowgoat to the market and was gone all day.

Grunhilda became so hungry while she waited, she started eating some of the dry wall of their cottage.

Finally, as the night closed in, Jaqueline arrived home – minus the snowgoat.

"What did you bring me Jacq?" Mother asked, her mouth watering as she anticipated the feast the snowgoat must have been bartered for.

"I have the answer to all our problems," Jacq said. "My pockets are full of magic beans! We will grow them and roast them and turn them into a hot beverage that people will come for miles around to savour. People will laugh at how we misspell their names on the cups and we shall be the talk of the town."

Jacq held out a handful of beans to show her mother. They were small, brown and boring looking.

Grunhilda took one of the beans and bit it, then rolled it around in her mouth before spitting it out. "Fye! You idiot! You were supposed to get food! You sold our snowgoat for a handful of stupid beans!'

Jacqueline said, "If you wanted to sell the goat for *specific* things, you could have gone and done it yourself, not made me do it while you sit here and do nothing and then complain about the results."

"Fo! What did you say?"

"Nothing." Jacq said. "I'll be in my room."

"It's not there any more, I ate it," Grunhilda said. "Don't roll your eyes at me. Fye! You would have done the same!"

Jacq was now hungrier than ever, so she nibbled a few of the beans. They were bitter and strange, but at the same time, somewhat invigorating.

She set to work following the instructions the marketwoman had given her. Crushing the beans until they had the texture of fine soil.

Thankfully they had water dripping from the hole in the roof, so she collected the raindrops in a metal pot - one of the few things her mother couldn't eat.

The water boiled as it sat on top of their metallic, and therefore non-edible, stove.

"Fo! What's that smell?' Ma asked, with a hungry look in her eye.

"Our change of circumstance," Jacq said, serving up a cup of the brown brew.

They both sipped it and agreed there was *something* special in this water.

"This is giving me life!" Mother said. "I feel like I can get things done. I also feel like talking quite a bit now, and quite fast, how interesting this is don't you think? Can't imagine I'll get much sleep now."

Jacq ran to their neighbours and asked if they could get some milk from the cow.

What with one thing and another, Jacq and the neighbour agreed to pool their resources. Soon they created creamy brown hot drinks and people from all over town followed the delicious aroma to Jacq's cottage stoop.

Life improved dramatically for Jacq and Grunhilda. They soon had enough money to buy more beans to turn into drinks, and a little leftover to fix the roof and buy back some of their furniture!

Such was the quality of the creamy brown drink, people in the town became more productive and developed a unique dialect that included talking incredibly quickly. Life was good.

Chapter Two

People came from far and wide to Jaq's small town to drink this magical elixir. Some people added honey, others wanted a dash of plütz in theirs. However they wanted it, Jacq made it just how they liked it.

Everything was going so exceptionally well!

And then one morning, Jacq woke up early to get the water boiling and the brown bean drink brewing, but there were no customers.

"Fum! That's odd", she thought, as she walked out of the cottage to make sure she hadn't accidentally opened in the middle of the night.

And that's when she saw it.

A giant new company had come into town and set up an enormous brown bean brewing shop directly across the laneway from her cottage!

"What's this?" Jacq walked into their store to see all the townsfolk in here. The same people who often came to her cottage stoop to buy a cup of bean brew. Now they were sitting around drinking someone else's brew.

There was something very strange about the looks on their faces, as if they were all under some kind of spell.

There was music playing in the room, which sounded so lovely. It was a harp, and it was playing all by itself, as if by magic!

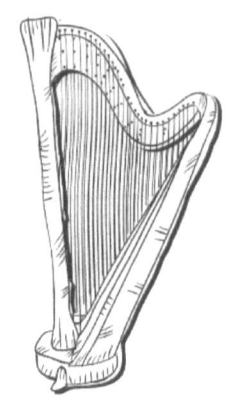

"What's in these beans?" Jacq wondered, as she ordered her own cup and had a sip. She was probably jealous, but all the same she was sure the drink didn't taste as good as her own variety of brown water.

Feeling confused and upset, Jacq went home to think of ways she could defeat this brown bean giant. She also had to think of ways to use up all the leftover milk she hadn't sold. One thing for certain, it wouldn't go back into the neigbour's cow!

She had a few customers that morning, and the next, but after a several weeks, hardly anyone came by any more. They preferred the giant's shop, and weren't interested in visiting Jacq's quaint brown water stoop where they had to stand around outside.

Then came some really bad news. Jacq's neighbours could no longer supply her with milk – they'd sold their cows to the giant.

'This giant is killing our town!' Jacq said.

Having previously lived in poverty, and feeling as if she were only just starting to trade her way out, there was no way Jacq was going back to being hungry and poor again.

Only one thing to do – she had to go and work for the giant.

Chapter Three

Months passed. Life became even more difficult. In the giant store, the harp played all the time in the corner. Sure, it was lovely, but the harp tended to only know a few classic melodies, so they were often on repeat. This was fine for visitors who only spent half an hour or so in the store, but it started messing with Jacq's head to hear the same tunes over and over and over and over and … you get it.

Then something *really* terrible happened.

The water supply to the town no longer worked. One morning, Jacq would take a bucket to the well, crank the handle and pump up some fresh cold water for drinking, cleaning and bathing. The next, the pump ran dry.

People rubbed peppermint over their arms and heads in order to hide the smell. Fee! Fye! Fo! Fum! Everyone could smell the toil of the Brugelians! It was bone-grinding work just to make enough to pay for a little bread. Or as the locals shortened it: *They ground their bones to make some bread.*

As if by magic, the bean water store still had a reliable water supply. People came from far and wide to buy water in small cups and half-buckets.

Sure, Jacq had a job and had food, but she couldn't shake the feeling that life was being pretty unfair to her and everyone else right now.

It was Jacq's responsibility in the brown bean store to clean all the tables and then wash and dry all the towels. The customers often didn't see her do it, so they didn't appreciate it, nor did they leave her any tips.

One night, after scraping the dregs from the bottom of the bean brew barrels, Jacq found a notebook left behind by the manager. On the front was a picture of a chicken sitting on a nest of golden eggs, which was pretty unusual.

Of course she opened it (otherwise there would be no story development!) and read page after page of information which could make her wealthy beyond her wildest dreams. For a start, every recipe used in the store was in the book, along with the method used to make the maximum amount of brown brew from the least amount of beans. But the really juicy bit was the signature from the town mayor beside a secret agreement to divert all the town water to the bean brew store!

At last, she had the knowledge to slay this giant! Jacq threw the recipe book and the harp into a sack and ran home to her mother. She didn't have far to go, because it was just across the pathway, but it felt like her legs were burning by the time she reached the door.

Jacq dropped her sack and returned with an axe. "Follow me, mother!" she called out behind her shoulder, and ran back to the giant shop across the street. There she attacked the water pipes which were sucking the town dry.

Whack, whack, whack! Went Jacq.

The townspeople heard the chopping and came to investigate.

"Our town water supply didn't dry up, it's in here, they've been stealing it from us all this time!" Jacq cried.

But everyone was confused, because they'd lived quiet lives and had never engaged in public rebellion or community activism. They didn't know what to do or where to look.

Suddenly Jacq's axe cut through the pipe. Water sprayed everywhere!

It sprayed up into the sky, creating a beautiful rainbow. It sprayed across the street, turning the pathway to mud. It sprayed downwards into the cart-park, making a lake.

The townspeople may not have known much about civil disobedience, but they knew the value of water. They raced to grab buckets and pots and mugs of all sizes, to save as much of the water as possible.

People played in the water, even though it wasn't much of a sunny day. But also, hardly any of them had been able to bathe and clean themselves for the longest time, so it cheered them to get a good soaking.

Then Jacq had another brilliant idea – the first really good idea since selling the family snowgoat for those bags of beans at the start of the story.

She handed out towels for everyone to use, and they were so grateful they came to her house the next day and brought plates of food and hand-crafts and thickly knitted scarves as way of saying 'thank-you'.

With no guaranteed water supply, the giant store closed down.

Jacq went back to brewing up her beans every morning. Her customers soon returned to her cottage stoop, because they discovered that not drinking the bean brew every morning gave them all terrible withdrawal headaches, and Jacq made such a lovely brew.

And everyone lived caffeinatedly ever after.

Grand Duchess Elmaree

ELMAREE, BORN UNDER A TREE. SITS ON A
THRONE WHERE A BOY SHOULD BE.

The following story is an historically accurate account sourced directly from the diary of Grand Duchess Elmaree. Entries have not been edited to correct spelling or the uncooperative tensing of verbs. This was one of the main reasons for The Brugelian Historical Society expelling two members, who went on to form the Historians' and Grammarian's Guild of Brugel (two historians, one of whom also identified as a grammarian.)

This is a tale of loss and sadness. A tale of a broken country and, on a more personal level, broken hearts. It does not end well for our protagonist. It's why this story is not at the very end of this collection — why entertain

readers for hours with wit and charm, only to end on a downer?

History cannot be cheese-coated. Despite having the best advisors, loyal staff and a resourceful mind, Elmaree did not win. Through no fault of her own, she lost her country and she lost her throne. It's important to state this up front, just in case you're holding out hope for a happy ending. There isn't one.

Born in 1724, Brugelish scholars claim Elmaree was most likely born very soon after her parents married. Possibly within a few minutes of them completing their vows. (But at least they were complete!)

Her mother, Flora Venzelemma and father, Grand Duke Savo, had married under a 'Wedding Elm' in the palace gardens; a long-standing Brugelish tradition which continues to this day.

The belief that Elmaree was born 'en plein air' is most likely apocryphal, but it fits with the rhyme so people believe it. Plus, it's in her name, isn't it?

Grand Duchess Elmaree was the first woman to rule Brugel, from 1740, which was a perilous time in Brugel's history.

In hindsight, there were a great many perilous times in Brugel's history, but the 1740s did seem particularly difficult for whomever was unlucky enough to be in charge at the time.

For example, if you find yourself sitting in a food court at lunch time and some noisy louts move in and take up all the tables around you and pick on you for your food and beverage choices – well, you get up and move somewhere quieter, don't you? In Elmaree's case, the food court was the map of Europe and the 'noisy louts' were the Slaegalese and Russians on an expansion spree. It's very hard to pick up an entire country (no matter how small) and move somewhere quieter. Plus, in this food-court-of-Eastern-Europe scenario, some of the people on the smaller tables joined in with the noisy louts, making this particular lunchtime (and laboured analogy) incredibly strained for all concerned.

Grand Duchess Elmaree's Diary

Wednesday, 13 December, 1741

The days grow short, the leaves are falling in great drifts every time a tree sneezes. The air is strong with burning pine and bruge-loak. Fires roar day and night to shoo the damp away.

We have a problem, and I don't mean the weather. Having reached the age of adulthood, everybody recognises it's high time I marry. Being a Grand Duchess, I must marry someone who will help Brugel form a strong alliance. Someone who can bring extra trade and a defence force or three.

Today we must look at options, even though I do not relish the thought of marriage. Being a Grand Duchess means it's not my will that matters. It's what's good for Brugel. How apt that we hold the discussion on a Wednesday, a day popular for weddings.

I sit at the head of a table in our long room, my cleverest, sharpest, most experienced advisors all around. I'm sure by the end of this session we shall have a way forward. Or at least a way to hold my greedy neighbours at bay for a little longer. The following is a record, as best I can remember it.

"Thank you for coming here, I appreciate your wisdom in this delicate matter." It's a good start, don't you think?

The advisors all nod and Daria Escu says, "We serve at your pleasure, Grand Duchess."

I do enjoy when they call me Grand Duchess. It has a lovely ring to it. Daria is always so respectful to me. As she often speaks first, she sets the tone for the others to follow.

"Let's not beat about then. I'm eighteen and eligible. I need to make an alliance with someone, otherwise, to put it bluntly, Brugel is at risk of invasion. Plus I need to make a few heirs. Who do we have?"

The advisors look at each other, but nobody says anything. What are they scared of? I won't bite their heads off. "Come on, I'm not getting any younger!" It's not as if I am looking forward to marriage. From all accounts it is unpleasant but necessary.

Ilinca Niscu says, "We are having difficulties finding eligible bachelors, Your Grace." Ilinca is trustworthy and speaks bluntly, which I value.

"Really?" That's new to me. I thought there were dozens. "There are plenty of countries around here.

Surely one of them has an unburdened bachelor to be my consort?"

Miklos Bencic says, "This is where the difficulty lies, Your Grace." He coats his words with soft feathers, fearing I will be crushed by the weight of reality. "Some have displayed interest." Then he stops, as if I'm expected to extrapolate more from that.

Ilinca clearly sees my confusion. "I believe what is happening is we have interested parties, but only if you are *their* consort, not the other way around."

That makes me so cross! "They're scared of me, aren't they? Gods forbid a woman should have a brain and use it! Surely there's a Prussian or a Russian *Tsarling* who wants a change of climate?"

Daria gently clears her throat. "Your Grace, Russia does have Tsar Ivan the sixth. He is unbetrothed."

"Fine then, what's he like?"

Daria blushes red. "Ma'am, he wears diapers."

"What?" The floor wobbles beneath me at the thought of a grown man needing such assistance. "How in-bred is he?"

"Oh no, Ma'am, he's all there, as far as we can tell. It's just that he's barely a year old."

A groan escapes and I stare at the ceiling, silently counting to ten so I can pull myself together again. "You're enjoying this, aren't you?"

After a while, when nobody else says anything useful or practical, I look to each advisor in turn. "What? What is it you're not saying?"

Nobody wants to speak.

"Come on, out with it."

Sorina Popa eventually clears her throat. "Your Grace, we feel there are difficulties finding a suitable alliance because of the … um … rumours."

Everybody else nods, but kept their mouth shut. There's a palpable sense of relief playing over their faces, because somebody has finally said it.

"I could play dumb and ask, 'what rumours?' and 'what are you talking about?' but that would insult us all. It's my archery lessons, isn't it? They are scared of a woman who can defend herself?"

Daria clarifies. "Not so much the *lessons*, Ma'am … but about … your *tutor*."

If this isn't the most ridiculous double-standard I've ever encountered, I don't know what is. Frustration has me counting silently to ten. "He is the most skilled archer in Brugel. Would you have my skills suffer simply because he is an attractive man?"

Now that I think about it, Leopold my archery instructor is rather good looking. But that's because of his fitness and confidence, which comes from being so very good at what he does. If my tutor were plain and weak, he'd be useless!

As one, the advisors look shocked and confused. I don't imagine I could get a more quizzical reaction than if I'd decreed the moon was inhabited with ferrets.

Daria speaks for all of them, in her continued

respectful way. "Your Grace, it's not quite that simple. You see the rumours are a little more, ah, *detailed* than that. Some of the eligible bachelors who have not completely ruled out an alliance, are otherwise waiting to see if you are already with child."

My face instantly heats from within. No words come, only spluttering. "Is that why they ... of course it must be ... do they think I'm desperate or something? Heavens above, hells below and snowgoats in the middle. What a mess!"

Daria adds, "Of course, we know it's impossible. We have stated that."

I have to slow my breathing. "Do they respect me so little they would share this rumour so openly?"

Miklos keeps his voice low and asks, "Are you?"

"Oh dear!" Will I ever stop blushing and spluttering? "Of course not! I shouldn't even have to say that." I can't believe anyone here would even need to ask. "But here we are!" What hope is there for me?

I can't remember much more of the meeting, only that those stupid rumours are spreading. I hadn't even thought about it, because he's my archer – he's there to do a job and he trains me well. I have done no wrong!

It's true what they say, rumours dance about the hillsides before the musicians have time to unpack their instruments.

If only my father were here – but of course he is not. But if he were here, he'd be making the big decisions and nobody would dare say such rude things about me. Because he would be the Grand Duke and I would be but his loving daughter and anybody spreading rumours would have to deal with him!

My mother, Flora, does her best, but she was never raised for this level of duty. She too has rumours dancing about the hills – one is that she borrowed her name from the city of Venzelemma itself, because she had no real family to speak of.

People are so cruel.

And the more these rumours spread, the more they become accepted and the less I am respected.

I need to be strong and fit, archery is but one of my fields of endeavour. I can ride and jump, thanks to years of training, and have a strong flock of champion snowgoats because I know how to breed the right animals to produce a healthy litter. I have also perfected the skills for making iced cream, courtesy of the palace chefs. Nobody has started rumours about them … have they?

Friday, 15 December

Why did they tell me about those ridiculous rumours? This morning when I had my regular archery practise with Leopold, I found myself blush-ing! My gullible advisors have put the silly idea in my head that I am already carrying his child! And because of this, the suggestion has grown like a weed in my fertile imagination. Drat and bother! I had to call the lesson short. I'm embarrassed with how poorly I treated Leopold as well. He did not deserve that. Of course he is a handsome lad. I was aware of that. But now these silly rumours are sprouting and I cannot help notice just how *very* handsome he is. This is so silly. I am a sensible young woman! Why is my blood pounding at the thought of my next lesson?

Monday, 18 December

Today's archery lesson contained more fumbles than a cat juggler on a snowgoat. I had to stop early and retire indoors (and I do so enjoy being outdoors.) This would never have happened if my advisors hadn't raised 'the archer issue'.

In the end, I had to confess to Leopold the true reason my aim was so poor.

"This is completely not your fault, and you have only ever been a capable and talented tutor," I started to say, as I aimed at the target, trying to get it over with, while still training somewhat.

He said plainly, "Is this about the rumours?"

I loosed the arrow and it sailed badly to the left, missing the target entirely. I'm supposed to be getting better, not worse.

Leopold said, "I'll take that as a yes."

I set another arrow and drew back. "They are most vexing. And untrue, of course."

"Of course, Your Grace. Get your elbow higher if you can."

"And you see," the arrow flew, hitting the edge of the target. At least it was getting closer. "I never realised people were saying such things. And they are making assumptions just because," I drew back another arrow and held my elbow higher, as he instructed, "we are two young people."

Leopold said, "Your advisors are welcome to join your lessons, then they could see there is absolutely nothing to be concerned about."

"Nothing?" The arrow flew badly again. So much for the raised elbow. "Not even a little?"

He guided my arm for the next shot, and despite the cool winds and deep snow all over the hillside, his hand left warmth along my skin. "Your advisors are at this very moment looking out the window, determined to catch any sign of even the most lukewarm signs of romantic involvement. They will find none."

As reassurances go, that was downright insulting!

My body tensed so much the arrow flew completely over the target. "Then how do you do it? I'm getting flustered and stupid merely having this conversation. You're the very definition of calm. How do you contain yourself? Am I not the most eligible young woman in Europe?"

"Of course, Your Grace. But I guarantee you I shall make no outward sign of it."

"None at all?"

"I packed my buckskins with snow, Your Grace."

Involuntarily, my eyes darted down. He erupted with laughter. Cannot believe I fell for it!

Thursday, 21 December

The end of year festivities are bringing joy to Brugel, despite the continuous snowfall. I worry about the bridges collapsing under the weight of it all, but I look out the frosty window and see people clearing the streets and riding snowgoats. They seem happy, although they must be so terribly cold.

Saturday, 23 December

Everybody from High Orthodox to Low Pagan is busy celebrating the festive season. The streets are filled with music. Pretty decorations adorn the front doors of houses and businesses. The air is redolent with the smells of mulled wine, roasting Brugelnuts and bleating snowgoats.

There was box left behind in my receiving room this afternoon. I opened it to find a leather arm guard for archery practice. Tucked inside it was a note saying, 'Elbow up,' but was unsigned. I know who it was anyway.

Shattering this joy comes the most hideous news.

Messengers have somehow made it through the incredibly deep snowdrifts to inform us that baby Ivan the Sixth's second cousin, Yelizaveta, has staged a coup and locked the young Tsar in the cellar with his immediate family. Yelizaveta is now the Tsarina, apparently.

At least the heavy snow will protect Brugel from invasion until the new year. Nobody in their right mind would try to attack in such weather.

Wednesday, January 3, 1742

Did I suggest nobody in their right mind would invade in this climate? It was the truth, for somebody completely soaked in madness and bloodlust is at this very moment looking greedily upon Brugel - and my soul - as his next conquest.

Prince Faddei of Slaegal is but five and twenty. I don't know why people say it like that, it's so much faster to say twenty-five is it not? Yes, I am procrastinating whilst writing in my diary, because I cannot yet accept what is happening.

Faddei's barbarism is legendary in these parts, having already slaughtered the hetmannis of Craviç and wiped the principality of Schlossduff-Danderr off the map.

He has sent me an 'invitation'. It's a demand. I could write it all here but I'm not in the mood to humour him. He has given me a deadline of Wednesday, February 14 to accept his proposal of marriage.

Delightful!

Friday, January 5

We moved my archery lesson inside as the snow is simply too deep and daylight hours too fleeting. With the fires roaring and the tables and chairs moved to the side of the long hall, it makes for a well-lit target, with no concerns for cross-winds.

Being indoors, many more can join in, and they do. This is excellent as they will see for themselves there is nothing of concern happening between Leopold and myself.

Leopold charms everyone. He guides the women's arms into the right position and fills their ears with praise. For the gentlemen, he offers advice when asked and dignified but not effusive congratulations when they do well. If only he were rude and sarcastic, it would make disliking him so much easier.

When my turn arrives, I am wearing the new glove. He either didn't notice or deliberately did not look. How is he so composed?

He says, "Remember to breathe slowly and loose the arrow between heartbeats."

How did he know my heart was racing? I nock the arrow, hold my elbow high, breathe out slowly and let loose.

Goatseye!

The hall erupts with cheers.

If I marry Faddei, the hall will erupt with their blood.

Best keep that information to myself and not ruin the mood, then.

Monday, January 15

One month until Faddei's demand expires. This is quite terrible. I am not hiding out, not really. It's just that the iced cream cellars are further from the castle than even the archery range. It is near the lake, and staff have packed the cellars with sheets of ice and blocks of snow. Shrouded in thick furs and layers upon layers of clothing, I sit here eating my tumultuous emotions.

Perhaps if I eat too much, my body shall freeze and I will not have to marry Faddei.

Obviously I have written this later, back in my chambers. I would not have been able to write in the cellars – the ink would freeze in the bottle, as would my clumsy fingers.

Yes, yes, I must get on with the important thing that happened today. I'm not even using very good grammar. I am delaying, again, because I can scarce believe what took place. So I shall not start a new paragraph in case it is too easy to read amongst the rest of my ramblings, but Leopold entered the iced cream cellar whilst I was there and long story short, my brains and heart are no longer my own.

"There you are!" He says, cheerful as a bluefinch in spring. Then quickly adds, "Your Grace."

"Are people looking for me?"

"No search parties as yet, but they'll notice you missing from the dinner table soon."

"I'm not hungry."

He surveys the empty barrels but does not correct my obvious lie. "You don't have to stay in here, the iced cream will not melt on the way back to the dining room."

"Fine. Yes, I admit I am hiding out here because I cannot face the court."

He takes a seat, clearly not about to leave me alone. "I missed you at archery training today."

This barrel is now empty, so I leave it on the floor and reach for another stacked nearby.

He says, "I hope the glove has helped a little."

I spin around. "It *was* you! Why didn't you say anything when I wore it?"

"Too many people watching. I felt it best to say nothing, lest it embarrass you or feed more rumours."

Drat him for being so thoughtful. I crank the lid off a fresh barrel. "Ohh, this one has roasted coffee beans." I have only the one spoon, so I wipe it on my arm to clean it off. "Want some?"

He accepts the spoon, ladles some iced cream on it and eats it. His face softens with something approaching rapture. Then he wipes the spoon clean and hands it back. "A fitting last meal."

I dig in far less politely and scoop as much iced

cream as the spoon will hold. "Wait, what 'last meal'? Why do you say that?"

"I think it best I leave the palace. You need an archery instructor who will not subject you to gossip."

He's leaving me? I stare at him, spoon hovering in front of my open mouth. "But that's not fair!" How very un-Grand Duchessy of me. I think I then ate a massive amount of coffee bean iced cream in a storm of confusion.

He gives me the saddest expression. "As long as I'm here, the rumours will not leave. And I cannot allow my feelings to play havoc with state business." He coughed, clearing his throat. "I have tried to keep my emotions and feelings submerged. To my everlasting regret, I have not achieved this. Your Grace, anyone who spent more than five minutes in your company would come to admire you for your wit, your salt-laden sarcasm and your *mnb*."

"My what?"

His eyes flew wide and he pointed to his throat.

Oh dear heavens! He was choking!

I dropped the spoon and the iced cream barrel. I grabbed him around the chest and pulled him in to me, blowing the wind out of both of us. I'd seen some-thing like this work with the ladies in court, who held their babies and patted them on the back to get their wind out.

No luck, he was still choking!

He drew his arm up, bending it sharply at the elbow-

Of course! Elbow up! I dropped one knee in front of him, then pulled my elbow back, high and sharp, catching him directly in the stomach. He barked out a cough. The coffee bean flew out of his throat, pinging against the barrels and skittering onto the floor.

Leopold crumpled in exhaustion, gulping icy breaths. Tears sprang from his eyes as he bent over.

"Elbow up did the trick," I said.

He coughed and spluttered and shook his head, still gasping. "Was pointing to my back," he demonstrated again, putting his elbow up so his hand was close to the space between his shoulder blades.

Cheeseballs and shakers! How did I get that so wrong? Although it had worked. "I'm so sorry!"

"Don't be. I've never been so glad to be beaten up!"

"I did not mean to hurt you."

"Good use of the elbow."

"You taught me that."

We were both on the freezing stone floor. And I shall procrastinate again as I recall whether I am writing this is present tense or presently recalling the immediate past. But the reason I'm filling lots of words here is because something wonderful and also a little bit terrible but mostly brilliant happened. I had a cloth in my coat pocket, one of my mother's. I always carry something of hers with me. I handed it to Leopold to wipe his face, and he rejected it in favour of using his sleeve. He didn't want to dirty it. And now I have written enough words to disguise the contents of what happened next and punctuation be damned because I was still holding him, or somehow my arms were on him and I was rubbing his back or something and then I'm not sure if I was moving just to keep us both warm in this Arctic cellar. He said I'd saved his life which was probably true, but I'd also put his life at risk by him finding me in here and what with one thing and another we were kissing and I'm fairly sure it was mostly my idea. I pulled him in close, as close as our bulky coats and layers of furs would allow. I had to use my teeth to get my gloves off. Hands free at last, I held his face. "I am so glad you're alive. That was terrifying to watch."

"It was terrifying to experience."

Now I am breathing hard, but I'm not the one who nearly choked to death in a freezing cellar that could so easily double as a morgue. "I thought I'd lost you. If it's all the same, and I know you're still getting your breath back, but I really need to kiss you now."

He smiled. "All things considered, is that a good idea?"

"You don't want to kiss me?"

"I want to kiss you more than take my next breath."

That sealed it. I closed the distance and planted my mouth onto his and our cold skin heated on

EBONY MCKENNA

contact. It was a terrible place to kiss. Not the lips, obviously, but the cellar location. Our breaths caused plumes of steam and our eyelashes clumped with crystals. But the kiss was so lovely I didn't care so much. When I pulled back, I had only one eye that would open. He had to peel his apart.

Leopold looked at me with such reverence I nearly cried. He said, "This is not the best environment in which to explore romantic feelings." Then he added, "Your Grace."

"We should continue this somewhere warmer." I said.

He looked at me, his face fell. "Please, Your Grace, I cannot put you in such a compromising situation. Your reputation and the very future of Brugel is at stake."

"I don't care, and last time I checked, I was the one kissing you." I kissed him again, our lips meeting so perfectly, as if we were created only for each other.

He pulled away and said, "You will care when it all turns to mud."

"Do you regret our kisses?"

"Never. But Your Grace, this cannot continue. You must marry Faddei."

We kissed again, because it was so very delightful. Why think about tomorrow or next month when such kisses are happening right here and now?

After a good long time, we pulled away. I had an

idea. "What if I'm already married? Then I can't marry Faddei because I would no longer be able to."

"Then he will sack Venzellema and destroy Brugel."

I already knew this. "But … after I marry him, what do you think Faddei would do to Brugel, or me?"

Leopold sighed deeply, sending out more plumes of steam. "He will sack Venzelemma and destroy Brugel."

"If Brugel is doomed either way, why shouldn't I marry right now and get to choose my husband?"

Things became very quiet for a little while, until he eventually spoke. "Who would you choose?"

Isn't that obvious? "You of course."

"The cellar has frozen your good sense. As flattered as I am, we both know that's not a good move. I bring no lands, no armies and no great treasury. It would be a foolish match."

"My mother brought no fortune to her marriage either."

He stopped arguing with me and we kissed a little more. Until he had to go and ruin it by bringing reality back and urging me to either make another alliance or go ahead with Faddei, and pray the brute was as clumsy as he was bloodthirsty.

I said, "After Faddei dies, by some miraculous accident, I then get a husband of my own choosing?"

"That's generally how it works."

"It's something to think about. He does bring an army, treasury and lands."

"Precisely."

"Alas, there is a flaw in this. What's to stop Faddei murdering me on our first night?"

Friday, February 9

Ever since the kissing session in the cellar we have been extremely careful to never be seen alone together. All archery practise now happens in the great hall, with many students keen to benefit from Leopold's skills. He even flirts with some of my court to give the impression he is as carefree and unattached as the day he arrived. He did such a convincing job Daria approached me after morning coffee to ask if I was coping with the news he had formed an attachment with another lady. You should have seen how clueless I appeared. Leopold is such a fine actor, he has everyone convinced there is absolutely nothing going on between us.

I play my part to perfection, being so newly betrothed and all.

Faddei has sent an actual betrothal ring via messenger. (He apparently can't visit me in person?) He truly must think I am a child for the only finger it fits is the smallest. Let him underestimate me at his peril.

Wednesday, February 14

They stand there, that wall of wickedness dressed in human flesh, watching me lift the quill to sign my life away. The oleaginous diplomats. The serpentine maids-in-waiting. Willing me to give my country and my lifeblood to them for the price of a line of ink on parchment.

Oh cruel fate that has cast me into such depths! What is this thing they call free will, when the only choice I have is whether to lose my heart or lose my country?

For I cannot have both.

Does it make me a terrible person to put my heart first? I am so afraid I do not think a true decision is possible. Why, if we have a heart, are we not free to bestow it to our person of choosing? Why did the maker give us such feelings if we were not meant to use them?

They are staring at me, waiting for me. I dip the quill deeply into the blue ink and lift it, watching the thick drops fall from the nib. The drops remind me of blood. Royal blood that will be spilled no matter how events from this moment unfold.

Follow my heart, I will lose Brugel.

Follow my head, I will lose the only man I will ever love.

I cannot give myself to Faddei. The suitor whose

knuckles are caked in blood from dragging them on the cobblestones!

He terrifies me. He towers over me. He ignores me.

He could snap me like a twig.

The decision comes to me, like clear running water washing all away. Clarity of reason says Faddei will destroy Brugel whether we are married or not. If I refuse to sign, he will declare war. If we marry, he will dispose of me and consume my country.

They are holding their breaths, waiting for me to sign. My face gives nothing away as I lower the quill into the ink once again. My heart is racing as never before. I look to Faddei and execute the only weapon in my arsenal before all is surely lost.

That weapon is defiance.

I snap the quill. Dark blue ink spreads over my hand and blots the paper.

The room is in uproar. Everyone is shouting, questioning, crying, gasping.

All except Faddei, who looks at me with his face of stone. He must have known I would refuse. As if he were waiting for it. He will lasso the moon and use it to crush the house of Brugel, of that I am certain. But the act is done. I cannot take it back.

My actions may spell death for everyone in this room and yet it is the only choice I had.

We are all doomed.

And yet. Somewhere, amongst this noise and mayhem, my heart sings.

Thursday, February 15

Faddei has set up a sizeable encampment on the other end of the Costeçi bridge. It is the widest and longest bridge in Venzelemma, with a slight rise in the middle.

His troops, there must be thousands of them, are standing around the multiple roaring campfires dotted all the way along the other side of the D'neep river. They sing loudly, their voices filling the skies with ballads of bloody victories and ghoulish triumphs, as powdery snow continues to fall.

Tomorrow, his troops will march across the bridge, and attack the city.

Tomorrow, the snow will be stained red with the blood of my people.

It is all my fault.

It is why I must flee.

If I am not on the other side of the bridge, ready to marry Faddei, as he demands, he says he will lay waste to the city. He came to Venzelemma to marry me, I have shamed him in front of his court. He must therefore destroy me.

If he'd been smart, he would have destroyed me there and then. Instead, he stormed off, then sent back a fresh list of demands.

Which has given the residents of Venzelemma time to flee. As I desperately wish to.

My armies cannot defeat Faddei. I have instructed many squadrons to remain sheltered tonight. They are carefully retreating - the noise of horses and wagons are muffled under the blanket of Slaegalese song and Brugelish snow.

We shall amass outside the city and regroup.

Yes, it's exactly as hopeless as it sounds.

A knock comes at the window.

"Leopold!" I whisper in delight as his handsome face appears under his furry hood. He has come to carry me away.

We embrace with equal measures of hope and fear. He helps me out onto one of the lesser balconies on the south walls, the ones facing away from the bridge. We are dressed darkly, but the bulky layers make this a slippery endeavour.

"Careful," he says, even though we are both being as careful as we can possibly be. I look for somewhere to place my feet on the stone balustrade.

I lurch and slip, he grabs my hand. "I said, 'careful'."

"Should the stones be this thick with ice?"

"The maids often throw the bathwaters this way.

It's all tuned to ice. You can't see it until you step on it."

"Why would they-?" An idea stills me. "We must get back inside."

"But we're nearly clear," he says.

"This will work, trust me."

The kitchen staff leap to attention, alarmed at my intrusion into their domain. They have every right to ask what I'm doing here. The weapons for warfare are within reach and they soon understand.

"Fill twenty samovars. Don't bother lighting them. Then wheel them to our side of the bridge."

They are not dressed for the cold, so I must wait. Impatience eats at me, so I write while waiting.

The thick snow muffles the trolley wheels as we pull the samovars along the street. We have not lit fires on our side. Faddei's troops will struggle to see us in the darkness. May their confidence be their undoing.

Leopold and I wheel the first samovar, slowly and carefully, as far towards the middle of the bridge as we dare. It takes four of us to lift the samovar onto the ground, then we dash back to get another. The kitchen staff are faster than us, and stronger, but I earn their respect for the plan and for doing some of the heavy lifting.

The singing from Faddei's troops intensifies. It

dampens the noise we are making as the last samovars are in place. Then Leopold and I turn the spigots.

I pray to the gods of all seasons that this works.

In the kitchens, we toast the helpful and loyal staff with plütz and leave them to their merry making. Then Leopold and I take every white tablecloth we can find to the nearby barracks.

The troops ask me, "What is all this material? Are we to make white flags and surrender?"

"Only as a last resort." I say.

We send word to the generals that our troops are to wait on our side of the bridge, but not advance. They are to keep the white tablecloths over their heads until the opposition reaches our side.

Leopold and I take it in turns not sleeping, as we wait with the troops for morning to come. I cannot tell if they regard my presence as a help or hindrance. At least I am here, they can see me. They have their swords ready and are sleeping where they sit in the makeshift barracks. The archers, who Leopold has trained personally, are waiting to move into position.

The singing from Faddei's side of the river ends with a triumphant, 'Hupp-Harr!' and the stomping of feet.

Then an eerie silence descends.

A small voice in my head reassures me, 'You have

done well, you did not run."

Another voice says, "I may still."

The sun has not risen, the clouds are still thick, snow is falling in heavy clumps. Watery light greets the day. There is movement and torchlight from the other side of the bridge.

Luckily I have not eaten, for my bowels will surely turn to water.

Speaking of water, the samovars have frozen in place on the bridge, but only a little of the metal is visible as all horizontal surfaces are covered in snow. With luck on our side, they won't see them or even work out what they are until they are upon them.

I only hope the horses don't suffer.

Our people are in their places, playing a freezing waiting game.

Whistles ring out from the other side. Faddei is on the move. Torches aloft in the gloom. They have burnt the rest of our bridges, the beautiful wooden craftwork now lost to history. This is a stone bridge, they cannot burn it. What good reason is the fire?

A message comes through from one of our lookouts.

The news takes many of us by shock. I did not see this coming, as I lack the imagination for such cruelty.

Yes, his people are marching across the bridge, everyone expected that. What we didn't expect was the size of the fires at the other end of the bridge … to stop his own people from retreating.

His confidence will kill them all.

Faddei's footsoldiers are at the front, marching and singing, confident of victory as they use shovels to clear the deep trenches required for the rest of the troops to cross. They sing and shovel, shovel and sing, making slow progress.

We wait, allowing them to become worn.

The singing is rousing and effective. They show no signs (or sounds) of tiring. They must have an endless supply of food. Or maybe it's plütz?

After multiple choruses, metallic clangs ring through the air as they hit something solid.

A samovar!

Laughter erupts on the bridge as the soldiers set about freeing the object. It slows them further. Excellent.

More shovelling follows, and then another rousing clang. This time they break the samovars out of the ice and out of their paths.

Everyone is holding their breaths. Or perhaps it is only I? They are digging snow on the downward side now. Is the snow so thick it is insulating them from the ice?

Is my plan doomed?

They make it past the rows of samovars and my heart cracks. We have failed.

No, it's worse than that.

I have failed.

They keep clearing snow, keep singing and keep

advancing on the downward slope. The icy slippery stones have failed to materialise.

I cannot let this happen. I must surrender to Faddei before my people are slaughtered.

It no longer matters that Leopold and I keep our relationship secret. The time for that is long past. Not caring who looks our way, I hold Leopold close and we share a parting kiss. "I will always love you. This changes nothing."

Before he can talk me out of it, I grab a cloak and walk out onto the street, knee-deep in fresh snow. It's more of a shuffle than a walk, because there's no way of seeing tripping hazards, so I must push my feet along the ground to clear the way.

My feet hit an upturned box. I push the snow off and stand up, so Faddei can see me.

"I accept your surrender," he says, from atop his horse.

"Give my people safe passage and you shall have it." It's not only the cold making my voice shake.

Faddei appears to consider this for a moment, then yells back, "No."

Then a beat later, he cries, "Charge!"

His soldiers dig furiously. Snow flies everywhere as they advance down the hill – until the digging gives way to yelling and confusion.

Can it be? The ice is finally making them slip. At least *that* part of the plan has worked.

"Get up, get up!" Faddei demands, but his people

are flailing and sliding, unable to fight the slippery conditions.

"Advance!" Faddei screams.

His mounted troops spur their horses on. They charge ahead, nostrils flaring, but only for a second. Then the horse's ears are back, eyes round and terrified as the ground slides away under their hooves.

The troopers and their horses slide down the rest of the way, unable to regain their feet.

This might just work! I scream towards the snow-covered land ahead of me, "Tablecloths away!"

My troops, who had been hiding under snow, throw off their covers and advanced on the confused and unsteady enemy.

Some of Faddei's troops stay to fight, others try racing back up the bridge, but their feet slide on the ice and they fall with sickening thuds. The horses are screaming in panic. They are crushing their riders and soldiers as they fall in sickening regularity.

It's hard to tell which delivers more injuries, swords or ice falls.

If Faddei hadn't set such huge fires behind him, they could have had a safe retreat.

But the battle isn't over yet.

Hand-to-hand fighting breaks out on the snow-covered street. Fighters on both sides slip and fall in the melee. Mud sprays on the snow ... except ... it's not mud. It's body fluids, causing fighters to slip and fall in all directions. I can't stand to look, yet it's my responsibility.

Arrows fly through the air. Leopold's archers stand on the balcony, firing down at the enemy.

What a hideous mess.

Faddei's troops are trying something new – they're using long hooks to grab the burning logs from their fires, then rolling them along the bridge to melt the snow and ice. They're also … pouring something onto the logs to keep them alight as they roll through the snow and ice.

It melts a clear path through our slippery ice trap, clearing the way for more of Faddei's troops to move in.

We're going to lose.

What a stupid fantasy to think I could survive this. That I could outsmart this maniac whose horses are at this very moment trampling over the bodies of his own soldiers.

Everybody is praying for a miracle.

The wrong gods hear our prayers. The sound of hoofbeats comes from the distance. Is this Faddei's reinforcements? Daylight shows their flag and it's worse than my darkest imaginings.

The colours of Yelizaveta Petrovna fly proudly, but she is not here to save me or form any kind of alliance.

That proverbial snowgoat slid away when she seized the throne from her nephew.

What I am sure of is that she is here to see which side is the victor; then she will attack that tired army and claim Brugel.

Even if we win, we lose.

I am going to hide this diary within the walls of the palace. I hope it is never found, for if it is, then the world, or at least Brugel, will learn of my utter cowardice. Leopold and I are about to flee into exile, disguised as ordinary citizens. Their shoes are so uncomfortable! I must leave everything behind. There is no more time.

Historians' note:

Brugel fell to Slaegal's Prince Faddei.

For four days.

Then it fell to Russia's Yelizaveta for fifteen years, until a popular uprising led by Elmaree's son Leopold, (named after his father) secured autonomy for Brugel. Because of Leopold the First's unusual heritage Brugel changed its status from a Grand Duchy to a Duchy. But at least they had their independence back.

Grammarian's note:

I'm really, really sorry.

Rudaba in the Tower

In a trading village by a river, lived a lovely young woman called Rudaba. She was cheerful and happy all the day long, because she was incredibly lucky in life. Her parents were merchants and business was good. She had avoided catching disfiguring plagues and poxes so far in her life, so she was very attractive. On top of everything else, she sang beautifully. Don't you just hate her already?

She had many friends she would sing with in a choir. They performed every week in the town square to raise money to help people who had been afflicted by plagues and poxes. This was during a very plaguey and poxey time, so choirs raising money were very much in demand.

One summer afternoon, after performing in the choir and raising quite a good sum of money from all the passing traders and shoppers, Rudaba became really, really hot. The singing on this particular day had been out in the full sun. Although quite beautiful, Rudaba's face and body perspired ferociously. She'd turned red and blotchy and her throat was dry.

She walked to the nearby river to splash water on her face. Alas, it wasn't cooling enough, so Rudaba unwrapped the metres of fabric around her hair and dunked her entire head in the river. It felt so good!

Back in these days, people had a very difficult time with their hair. It was hard to wash on a regular basis, because shampoo and conditioner hadn't been invented yet.

People with loose or springy hair, which flew this way and that, often caught nits and ticks. The little critters simply walked from one person's head to the next without much trouble at all.

The most hygienic thing to do back then was to wrap the hair tightly under a long cloth. Everybody, men and women and even small kiddies, but especially teenagers whose hair started getting really messy and oily and utterly embarrassing, would tie up their hair in elaborate wraps and rolls. That way, lice couldn't get in to make your life lousy.

Putting up hair in a wrap removed any pressure about appearances. There was no pressure about how often to wash hair, and if you were going grey or losing your hair, it didn't matter because nobody saw it anyway.

The only people who did get a glimpse of your hair were your immediate family, or, somebody who was about to join your immediate family, if you know what I mean. Yes, I mean that!

Rudaba sat on the rocks as the water splashed over them. She scooped the water into her palms and drank, then washed her face again. She stayed in the water until her whole body had cooled right down.

When she was ready to go home, she noticed another person in the river, splashing about and doing the same thing as she! He was about her age, about her height, and as she'd never seen hair like his before - because he too had let down his hair and dunked himself in the river - she couldn't help but stare.

He stared back, mouth open like a broken gate.

Finally he said, "I am so sorry for staring. Your hair is beautiful."

Rudaba said, "So is yours!"

Despite all that cool water, Rudaba's face suddenly became very hot again.

The boy grinned and looked away quickly, then dunked his head scarf in the water, getting ready to wrap his hair again.

Rudaba knew she shouldn't stare, but stare she did,

as the lad began wrapping his hair back into his scarf, tucking it in along the way.

Taking his time about it, Rudaba thought, as she too wrapped her own hair. Then had to start again because for some reason her fingers were not working the way they should.

When she looked up, the boy had gone, which was something of a relief, because he'd been standing right in the way of where she'd needed to walk, and it would have been embarrassing to have to move past him.

Feeling emotionally flummoxed at the strangely intimate, chance encounter, Rudaba made her way back home.

She slipped back into family life, but said nothing of the lad. When her family asked how her day had unfolded, she told them only of the singing and the heat.

Her parents were worried she may have fainted, as her face looked so flushed. Which would explain why she was so late home. She told them she must have lost track of time, and perhaps the sun had made her dizzy after all, because she wasn't hungry and wanted to go straight to bed up on the roof.

During summer, the families in this part of the world often slept on the flat roof of their houses. They lit a citronella candle in the corner to keep the mosquitoes away, and the evening breezes made it possible to sleep.

During the heat of this particular summer, Rudaba sang many more times in the choir in the heart of town, and the boy from the river came by to hear her. He placed coins and loaves of bread in the collection baskets, to show his appreciation and support.

After the choir had finished singing for the day, he smiled and waved to Rudaba, who waved back. They'd performed in the shade this time, so she wasn't as perspirational. The lad's smile (and generous donation to the pox and plague-afflicted townsfolk) impressed her.

And there's no denying it, he too was rather lovely to look at, having not been afflicted by pox or plague himself. Fate had dealt him a very good hand, with his lovely features, fine clothes and access to finance. Don't you just hate him already as well?

The lad said, "My name is Goshtasp. But you can call me Gosh."

"Gosh," Rudaba said, trying it out, "That's a lovely name."

"And in return, may I ask your name?"

"Oh, goodness, how rude of me, I'm Rudaba."

This made the lad smile, "That is a truly lovely name as well."

They both spent the next few minutes smiling and blushing at each other, like a pair of smitten twits.

Goshstap cleared his throat and said, "Rudaba, will you permit me to court you?"

Rudaba didn't know where to look! "Errrr," she hesitated, suddenly interested in her feet, "I don't know if I'm allowed to."

"Then I shall ask your parents for permission," he said. Then his face fell. "I mean, if it's all right with you, that is. This is completely your decision. No pressure whatsoever. Oh goodness, I'm rambling. It's just that I've never asked anyone if I may court them before."

Rudaba smiled so deeply her face hurt. Then she managed to form a few words, "That's fine, nobody's ever asked if they may court me before either."

They both smiled and giggled for a little longer, in that sickening way people sometimes do. Then Rudaba suggested they actually go to her parents' house because that seemed to be where things were leading.

Alas, when they reached Rudaba's family home, her parents were distraught. (This is an excellent development for storytelling, as events were going far too easily for our heroine and hero up until this point.)

Rudaba's parents were completely unimpressed. It did not matter that the lad had avoided poxes and plagues and was apparently healthy, nor did it matter about his wealth - although that was a definite advantage.

No, the problem was Goshtasp was the son of the family's largest trade rival. Rudaba and Goshtasp couldn't possibly form an alliance when the heads of both families were locking snowgoat horns over trade deals.

This was devastating news to Rudaba, who was rather looking forward to being courted. Whatever that meant.

It was also devastating news to the Goshtasp, who regularly worked with his father on those trade deals, and was now very scared of being accused of disloyalty to his father - and of sharing trade secrets.

What a mess!

Goshtasp left Rudaba's house a heartsick mess. "What were the odds of our families being such fierce rivals?" He asked Rudaba as she fare welled him at the gate.

"Quite high, when you think about it," Rudaba replied. "We are both from trader families, and we trade in medicines and other products, to keep us healthy and well fed, and we are of a similar social status. And the choir brings all the folks to the square. It was bound to happen, really."

The lad said on a sigh, "We were destined to meet and fall in love then."

"Oh!" Said Rudaba, "Are we in love already?"

"Not yet, true." Gosh said, "But that does seem to be where this is going."

"How is that?"

"Well, you'll keep singing in the choir, and I'll keep seeing you and hearing you in the town square. And on the next hot day we are bound to see each other down by the river."

"According to the cloud-readers (because weather forecasters hadn't been invented) we are in for some hot days next week."

"I will definitely be there, and if it's as hot as predicted, I will need to let my hair down."

Rudaba said, "That's a certainty on my part too."

"So you see, we truly are destined to fall in love."

Rudaba thought on this. "Goodness, it's almost as if we have absolutely no say in the matter."

Gosh said, "It's terrible. Free will is a mirage."

"What desperately bad luck we are now experiencing," Rudaba said. "May I give you a parting kiss, to relieve the ache that must be rending your heart at this very moment?"

Gosh said, "Yes please."

They shared a sweet, lovely kiss, full of angst for the potential heartbreak that would surely come.

And now we hate them a little less, for despite their previous good fortune in life, they were experiencing hardship, and the reader is experiencing a pang of sympathy for their situation, which, despite happening centuries ago, is so very relatable today.

On the next hot day, Gosh and Rudaba found themselves by the river, letting their hair down and sharing kisses.

It happened the next hot day after that as well!

When she returned home from yet another hot day requiring a visit to the river, Rudaba's father took one look at his soaking wet and thoroughly-kissed daughter and lost his temper.

"Gossip is spreading! My trade is suffering! Go to the roof right this instant. No dinner for you!"

Rudaba's mother, who understood the emotions of being a teenage girl so much better than her father, climbed the ladder to the roof and sat with her daughter. They talked for a while, until the stars came out. The citronella candles flickered, filling the air with lemony goodness.

"Your wrap is a mess," Mother said. "Come here and let me fix it."

As Mother pulled and untucked the fabric to start again, Rudaba let out a little "ouch" of pain. And then another.

"Sit still!" Mother said.

"I am, but why can't you be more gentle with my hair like Gosh is?"

Mother stopped and stared at her daughter. "You let down your hair for that boy, didn't you?"

Rudaba nodded.

Mother hugged her daughter. "This is the absolute worst time to fall in love. Father is struggling to secure trade deals and people in the town are talking. Can you not cool it until things get back to normal?"

"But I love him, Mother."

Mother sighed and said, "Of course you do."

Mother was mostly correct. Times were getting difficult for trade in the region. The latest delivery of medicinal herbs hadn't arrived as expected. Added to this, a recent donkeypox plague was making transport difficult. On top of all these woes, it turned out snow-goats were too small (and stubborn) to pull wagons, so the goods remained in the warehouses instead of being sold in the markets. Rudaba falling in love with their trade rival had become the straw that broke the prover-bial snowgoat's back.

Rudaba's parents were utterly exhausted as they set up their beds on the roof that night. The citronella candles were spluttering out, and many mosquitoes had bitten Mother on the face. One particularly big bite on her nose had turned pimply and red.

Rudaba couldn't sleep. Her heart yearned for Gosh, and the mosquito noises drove her mad. She swatted and smacked at them to drive them away, but nothing was working. Would she end up with a spotty face, like Mother? That mark on her nose was turning into a witch's boil!

She heard noises, they sounded like footsteps approaching.

Then something hit the side of the house.

Looking down from the roof, Rudaba saw Gosh throwing pebbles against her bedroom wall. "We're up here," she said.

"Hello up there!" He said.

"What are you doing down there?"

Gosh said, "Looking for you. My family is leaving town tomorrow, for the capital city. I could not leave without you."

"Have you come to take me away?"

"I guess I must be. If you will come with me. Completely your decision, of course. It's just that, if I am in the city, and you stay here, then we will never see each other again."

Rudaba said, "It hurts my heart to think that would be the case."

"Mine too, which is why I'm here," Gosh said.

At that point, Rudaba's parents woke up and demanded to know who she was talking to.

Panic flooded her. If they found her talking to Gosh, she would get into so much trouble, and she'd never see him again. But he was going to the city and she'd never see him again anyway. Oh why did these things have to be so dramatic? Why could they not have time to think things through and be sensible?

Rudaba's parents pulled the ladder up. "You're not going anywhere!"

Gosh called from below, "Let down your hair!"

Rudaba did just that. She unwrapped her hair and tied the edge of the wrap to the chimney, then abseiled down the outside wall.

She and Gosh embraced dramatically, because the moment called for it.

Her parents arrived a moment later, massively out of breath as they'd put the ladder back and climbed down. Plus, weren't as fit as they used to be.

"Mother, Father, I want to be with Gosh. I'm sorry you don't get along with his parents, but his parents are moving to the city now and so you won't have such trade competition anymore, so that's good news."

"Go," her father said, "One less mouth to feed."

"What?" Rudaba said.

"What?" Gosh said.

"What?" Mother said.

Father said, "I knew Gosh's father was relocating. But trade will still be difficult. So, Rudaba, it's either you leave with him, or he stays with us. With the way finances are going right now, it's better that you leave."

Rudaba said, "I was completely not expecting that. I had rather hoped you'd beg me to stay?"

"No time for sentiment. No doubt we will be in the city in a year or so ourselves. Trade in the regions is getting worse. If you're established in the city with Gosh, we'll have somewhere to stay when we sell up here."

"Oh," Rudaba said. "That rather takes the gloss off the romance, somewhat."

Mother said, "Your father does deals like this all the time. He's calling your bluff. If you want a life with Gosh, then go with him now. If not, stay with us. You're old enough to make your own decision, so make it."

Rudaba really didn't like the sound of that. "Can't you fight over me a little longer?"

Goshtasp said, "I've got it. Nobody else knows what's transpired here but us. We can say Rudaba was kept away from me, high in a tower. A terrible witch kept -"

"It's a mosquito bite!"

" -her away from everyone, until a brave prince climbed the tower and freed her."

Rudaba clapped her hands, "That's a great story, I love it. And can I be a lost princess?"

Mother said, "Come on Rudaba, we'll help you pack your things so you and Gosh can be on your way."

Satisfied that all would be well, and with the promise of being immortalised in story, Rudaba and Goshtasp made their way to the city and a new life together.

The Mother of Ashu

I n the sweet little hamlet of Ashu, lived a young woman called Nadejdna who was incredibly innocent. Neither her parents, nor her friends, had told her anything about married life. Yes, *that* innocent.

Luckily her husband, Vitali, was also innocent of married life. The two from Ashu really didn't have a clue.

Nadejdna's married friends dropped hints of course. One asked, "Are you expecting the stork to arrive one day?"

She replied "Why do I want a stork, are they especially tasty?"

"But my dear," and the woman took her into her confidence, "What are you doing in the evening, before sleep?"

Nadejdna replied, "My husband kisses me on the

forehead, then goes outside to pray by the Brugeloak tree."

"What is he praying for?"

"Babies, of course."

And so it went on, everybody hinting at the subject but never really explaining anything. This is what happens when everybody thinks somebody should be doing something, but nobody does anything.

Every day, one of her married friends would say something like, "Found anything under the tree today Nads?"

And Nads (for everyone began to call her that as Nadejdna was a little tricky to say, even for the Brugelese) would sigh and say, "I check the tree every morning, but no babies as yet. Perhaps I am not eating enough. It seems the mothers in the town are a lot plumper than I. Maybe that's what I'm doing wrong?"

And then one day, to Nadejdna's and Vitali's utter delight and surprise, there was a baby at the bottom of the Brugeloak tree!

The took the baby inside and sat in their warm kitchen, amazed with this miracle of life. A baby! The tree had worked! Nadejdna wrapped the baby in swaddling and went to her neighbours to show them the good news. Plus, she didn't have a clue how to look

EBONY MCKENNA

after the baby or how to stop her crying. And what was the smell? It followed her everywhere!

The neighbour, Oxana, decided it was high time Nads received some real advice, at least for the baby's sake. They spent the day together teaching and learning, learning and teaching. Then the next day, and the day after that. A few days later, as the baby girl began to thrive more and fuss less (but still made quite ghastly smells!) Nads found herself falling more and more in love with the baby.

Oxana asked, "Are you going to be able to give her back when the real mother comes forward?"

"What are you talking about?" Nads said, "I am her real mother. We found her under our tree."

Nads and Vitali were very happy parents, and took the baby with them every time they walked about the hamlet, just as the other parents did. They named her Liuba, which means 'Love' in Brugelish. They were very, very much in love with the baby and their little family.

Nads said, "I really love this baby. Should we check the tree again, to see if there are any more?"

Vitali shrugged and figured they may as well. They hadn't looked at the tree for a few weeks and he suddenly felt terrible that there might be a baby there, out in the open.

Imagine their surprise when they found not one, but two babies under the Brugeloak!

The babies were having a good cry and they both

needed a good wash as their swaddling was full. Vitali and Nads took the two new babies inside. Vitali milked their snowgoats with extra vigour to make sure there was enough for the babies. Then he thought about putting in an order for some more nanny snowgoats as they were likely to run out at this rate.

Their home in Ashu became very crowded and busy with three babies. Nads had to keep a diary (and name the next two babies) to keep track of their feeds and sleep times.

Word soon spread of the miracle Brugeloak tree where babies could be found. In the months that followed, Vitali and Nads found five more babies, bringing the total to eight.

Nads frequently sought the help from her neighbour Oxana. "I have so many children now, I don't know what to do. How do I stop getting babies?"

Oxana replied, "In most cases, I'd advise married couples to stop sleeping together."

Nads cried, "We are getting no sleep at all with these babies! And also, I need a new diary, and a couple more names. I have two boys that are called boy one and boy two because I don't know what to call them. Got any ideas?"

"Have you tried Vitali?"

"Yes, all three spellings."

"We'll need to read some more books in that case."

Eight babies in one year is a lot for anyone. Vitali and Nadejdna were finding things very difficult. The noise, the smell and the expense! They spent all their time looking after the babies and very little time making things to sell or trade. A few of their neighbours took pity on them and donated a nanny snowgoat and others stitched blankets and clothing for their growing family.

Nads was incredibly grateful for all their help. "I feel so foolish having so many children. And so close together! Perhaps we planted an especially robust Brugeloak?"

Every morning, Vitali would take his axe with him when he checked that Brugeloak, determined to cut it down. But then he'd get there and not find a baby, and feel badly for the tree, which provided so many edible nuts in the spring, lovely shade in the summer, pretty, compostable leaves in autumn and kindling in the winter.

Several more months went by with no more children, which was a massive relief. The babies were starting to crawl everywhere and get into everything. Nadejdna's answer was to swaddle them and hang them on hooks on the wall, so she could prepare food without tripping over them.

Just when they thought their baby discovering days were over, the babies started appearing again. In twos, threes, and sometimes fours!

It was getting seriously out of hand!

And yet the neighbours – and even some strangers – sent them food parcels and clothes to help them out. Some anonymous groups also sent building materials so they could build an extra room where the babies could sleep. (Not that they slept that much.)

Word of their incredibly large family spread far and wide. And it seemed the more people shared the story, the more babies they found.

Until one day, Vitali and Nads found five babies bundled under the tree. Vitali took the babies inside, then grabbed his axe and hacked into the tree.

It was such hard work, he had to stop and rest for the day. He'd finish the job later. Every time he found more babies at the base of the tree, he'd hack a little more away. Eventually, he pushed the tree over completely and hacked a flat surface into the tree stump.

The next morning, he found two babies lying on the tree stump. He fell to his knees and sobbed.

This is how their life continued for decades. Until one day, when they were in their sixties, the family received a summons to visit Grand Duke Javo of Brugel.

Nads said, "We can't go, there are not enough carriages to take us. You'll have to go on your own."

Vitali said, "I can't go and leave you. Yet it is exceptionally rude to refuse an audience with Grand Duke Javo."

Nads said, "The children who still live with us are getting so much bigger now, and they are helping around the house. I will get Oxana to send some of her oldest grandchildren over as well, to help out. Mariel and Juliel are both so very helpful."

And so, Vitali left to visit Grand Duke Javo. Mariel and Juliel came over to help Nadejdna and learn how to care for babies. They would be getting married soon, so they wanted to know what they were in for.

Nads said, "Married life is wonderful. Just don't pray so hard for babies, otherwise you'll end up like me."

Juliel said, (without thinking, obviously) "You know they're not yours, right?"

"Of course, they're mine! Whatever do you mean?"

Juliel turned a deep shade of red, having said something she should not have, even though it needed saying. "Granny told us word got out that you wanted children, so somebody who couldn't look after their own left them here for you to find."

Nads stared at the young woman, her mind reeling. "But, they're my babies."

"Yes, you took them in, but haven't you noticed that nobody else has so many babies?"

Nads chewed the inside of her cheek in thought and said, "Well, yes."

Mariel said, "Jules, we're here to help, don't upset her."

Nads was thinking out loud. "I was wondering when the babies would stop. None of my friends are having babies anymore, and yet I still am."

Mariel and Juliel nodded at Nads, waiting for her to put the pieces together. Then she burst out laughing and said, "My darling husband is … right this minute … having an audience with Grand Duke Javo! Oh, deary me! All this time we've been running an orphanage and I had no clue! Now, girls, tell me. Where do babies *really* come from?"

There was an old woman who lived in Ashu.
She had so many children and not one clue.
She gave them all clothes and goatmilk for dinner.
The neighbours helped out, which made her a winner.

LARA'S CHRISTMAS
GAMBLE

*In which we complete this delightful compendium with a
beautiful fairytale and a guaranteed happy ending.*

Chapter 1

"It's not stealing if I pay it back before they notice it's gone."

Lara Novak dashed along the narrow path through the forest. Her stays pinched. Normally her stays didn't pinch, but normally she didn't have one hundred silver schlipps sewn into the boning either. On this particularly foggy late November day, Lara's workmate Miss Jean kept pace with her, the infant Pavel hitched on her hip.

"I hope she comes." Steam puffed from Lara's nose as she tightened the shawl around her shoulders.

Miss Jean patted Pavel's soft head and cooed, "The witch promised she would, and witches always keep their promises."

Their steps crunched on the frosty ground. Ahead of them, the path opened out to a dirt road, where the damp air swirled and tried to make rain.

Late autumn in northern Brugel was full of quiet magic; delicate spider webs festooned with droplets of mist; brisk mornings and afternoons of watery sunlight; the milking shed filling with steam as the long-haired goats came in with bloated udders.

Soon it would get really cold, when the sun struggled to penetrate the dark clouds; when snow fell horizontally—and if it didn't snow, it rained.

Soon it would be the magical season of Christmas; but there would be no magic for Lara as another bleak year beckoned. Another year older and no prospects for a family of her own.

The lean months ahead was one reason why Lara's master, The Comte of Wistringia and his family had fled south to Craviç. The other reason went by the name of Napoleon, who was right now marching his armies east, directly through Brugel, on his way to somewhere else. [1]

Nearly all the servants had gone too, leaving scant staff to tend the animals. The family wouldn't return to the estate until spring, and only then if Napoleon had finished whatever it was he was up to.

Lara and Miss Jean were left behind on the estate, tending the animals. A precious few months of freedom to find Lara's true love and make their fortunes. Once they'd done that, they'd replace the schlipps they'd borrowed so that Comte Wistringia and his family would be none the wiser.

Ahead of her, Lara heard a wagon approach through the fog. She saw the muzzles of the two dark ponies, their flared nostrils snorting great clouds of steam. The blur of the painted, covered wagon came into focus, its rich dark timbers creaking as it moved along the road. It came to a stop next to Lara's path.

Taking a breath to steady her nerves, Lara stepped towards it and knocked on the door.

"You could have run home." A woman's muffled voice came from inside the wagon.

"Aye, and I may still," Lara said, her knees trembling from more than the cold. A now-or-never battle took place inside her as she debated whether to run.

The woman chuckled, a rich sound that reverberated inside the cabin and out into the surrounding trees. In summer, the noise would have startled the birds. At this time of year, the leafless boughs lay iced and silent.

"Come in child, let me tell your fortune anew," the woman said, as she opened the door and kicked down the riser so Lara and Jean could step in.

It was the same woman, Alishandra Orona, who had come to the servants' quarters last week. They'd given her fresh, warm milk; she'd read their palms. Her performance had been entertaining and enlightening, and now she was back. As she'd promised. Her painted face, curly dark hair, layers of shawls and colourful scarves cut a bright scene in the midst of the gloom. On her fat fingers sat every colour of jewel imaginable.

"I've not seen the likes in all my days!" Lara said as she took in the sight of so many gems. "I had no notion they came in so many shades."

Again the woman laughed as she helped them into a seat, sealing the door to keep the cold outside. The blend of rich, exotic fragrances assailed Lara's senses. How warm to be inside the wagon, cosy enough to remove her shawl and bonnet. Tendrils of her copper hair fell about her shoulders.

"They're not real jewels, child, though nearly as good. They come from a far-off city called Venice, where they make glass out of sand and they have rivers for roads."

"Oh be off with you!" Lara said. "Rivers for roads? All the horses would drown!"

The woman roared with laughter, then wiped away a tear of mirth as she composed herself. "But it's important, you see ..." she reached her palm out, inviting Lara to produce hers so the new reading could begin, "... Kylara Novak. You are a child of the light, but you are often times too hasty. Your true love is coming, but you will not recognize him at first."

"How did you know my full name?" Lara gasped—all the same she did not remove her hand, because the witch's accuracy made her keen to know more.

Beside her, wee Pavel gave a mewling cry. Jean cradled him under her shawls and quietly nursed him.

"You have the coins?" Orona asked.

"Yes, I have. Please look away so I may retrieve them."

The witch averted her gaze. Lara removed her top layers then unfastened the ties. With a few judicious rips of the fabric, she had the coins.

"… Ninety seven, ninety eight, ninety nine, one hundred," Orona counted.

Lara's pulse kicked up a notch. She'd just stolen a prince's ransom, for something she'd not even seen. For something that might not even work. Was this some elaborate theft? Would the witch kick them out of the wagon and disappear into the mist? No wonder she could afford to wear such incredible jewels.

But no, everyone knew witches never lied.

"You have kept your word, and now I shall keep mine," the woman said. She opened a soft fabric pouch and withdrew a delicate statue from inside. It looked to be made of nothing at all because Lara could see right through it.

"This is an enchanted faerie. She comes from the city of Venice, and she is made of glass so treat her with care. Take her with you, she will guide you to your one true love."

Breathing stalled as Lara took in the sight of the faerie. Then she gasped in shock as the heart of the statue began to glow red.

"She is bonding to you, Kylara Novak. Guard the faerie with your life. Do not give her to any other person, do not allow another person to keep her. When the heart of the fairy changes colour, your true love approaches. When she glows again red, you will meet me in this same place the following morning and return her to me. Your palm tells me you are a woman of your word, but I also see great cunning in you. Deceive me, and all that shall await you from now until the end of time will be sorrow and loneliness."

Three days later, the faerie nestled in Lara's pocket had yet to change its glow. No men had come into Lara's world. Correction: no *eligible* men. There was Schovajsa the warden, who spent his days patrolling the borders. [2] He also raised snow goats and had managed some success in local snowgoating competitions.

Then there was wee Pavel with his rosy cheeks, who mewled at his mother's skirts all day. A sly smile spread on Lara's face. They called Pavel's mother Miss Jean, despite the fact her belly had begun growing again.

"Don't fret Lara. The eligible men will come," Miss Jean confirmed as she slid the fillets of smoked trout away from the bones, "Schovajsa and I have seen to that."

"Are we doing the right thing?" A nagging doubt pulled at Lara's conscience. Stealing at any time of year didn't sit well with her, but stealing so close to Christmas made her feel even more of a sinner.

"Aye, and by the time the Master and his kin return, we'll be well-off," Miss Jean said.

"But the townsfolk will be poor," Lara countered as she dolloped the flatcake mix onto the pan and put it in the fire.

"We're not inviting the poor ones, are we lass? We only invite the ones what can afford it. This will be a winter to remember. We'll find a true love for you and make ourselves rich in the process."

---

1. At this very moment in history, Napoleon is of course on his way to Moscow, and certain defeat. He may have left France in Summer, but by the time he reached Russia, winter was well and truly upon him. Thus cemented the belief that Russia's greatest military weapon is her weather.
2. The warden's name, Schovajsa, meant 'he who hides by the river,' which suited him because he reeked like a stagnant pond.

Chapter 2

Her stays pinched. Normally her stays didn't pinch, but normally she didn't wear her mistress's stays. What were the Comtess's stays made of? Certainly not straw in the boning, that was for sure. They felt like *actual* bones. Each breath she took pushed her bosom towards her chin, but Miss Jean only glowed with satisfaction at the result.

"You'd pass for a real nob. Smile and keep the plütz flowing and today will be the first of many successful gatherings. Remember, they call it luncheon, not dinner, but after tasting Schovajsa's plütz they won't care anyway." [1]

A short while later the guests began arriving, all handing Lara a gold coin on entry.

Gold coins were worth so much more than silver schlipps. You could get at least fifteen silvers to each gold.

She showed them through to the guest lounge, which they'd turned into a games room. The sideboard groaned with food and decks of playing cards waited at the tables. Some tables also had dice, one had a board covered in a check pattern with small figurines. What had Miss Jean called it? Choss? Chits? …Chess! That was it.

Miss Jean tended the fire but other than that, she kept to the background and made sure wee Pavel stayed hushed in the kitchen. Doused in the Comte's cologne, Schovajsa stood sentry by the door to protect them from any trouble. The smell of goats still managed to break through his perfumed miasma.

While nobody was looking, Lara cast a glance at the statue tucked into the folds of her skirts. She and Miss Jean had added extra pins in her mistress's clothes to create a new pocket. The faerie's heart glowed purple—a new colour! It could only mean one thing; her true love was near. Perhaps he'd already arrived?

Casting a glance around the room at all the gentlemen, Lara wondered which would be 'the one'. They were all rather handsome and well turned out, and they'd all produced a gold coin, so that had to mean they had some fortune?

"To think, we could have done this last winter when we had so much trout we were sick of the taste of it," Lara said to Jean as she returned to the kitchen. "They're gobbling it all up. Better send Schovajsa back to the smoke house before we run out."

"Who would have thought nobs would eat common suppers?" Miss Jean said with a grin.

The games room hummed with guests, all declaring the food delicious, especially the soft cheese which went so well with the flatcakes and plütz. The gamblers played and laughed and smoked their pipes.

A cry rang out in the room, followed by gales of laughter,

"You win again!" the loser said.

A few moments later, Lara heard the words she longed to hear, as the loser issued a challenge: "Care to make it interesting?"

Oh yes, it was time to make this *very* interesting. Lara wanted to bolt to the table, but she made herself step leisurely towards the men, "Gentlemen, you are all having such fun. May I sit and watch?"

The men had the decency to blush at having a woman at the table, yet one of them fetched Lara a chair and she took a seat, sitting bolt upright in her unfamiliar stays. After a couple more rounds, she would play a hand herself, and that's when she'd start to make some *real* money. Plus, it allowed a chance to get to know some of the gentlemen, to find her true love.

Schovajsa and Miss Jean had taught her how to play the cards in summer, and she'd won their butter rations for a week. Now she'd win a lot more than that.

The players played on. Lara observed carefully.

Heavy footsteps suddenly rang in the hall.

Miss Jean smothered a cry of shock.

Schovajsa swore, his loud curse cutting through the air.

Lara bolted out of her seat to see the cause of the commotion.

Standing in the doorway, riding crop still in hand, was the Comte's youngest of five sons, Cezar. Mud flecked his riding boots and breeches, but it took nothing from his commanding figure as Lara took in his lean body; his riding coat fitting like a second skin and his broad shoulders seeming to fill the door frame. His eyes scanned the room with agonizingly slow composure, before coming to rest on Lara.

How he'd changed from their younger days, when they used to play together in the milking shed. Before class or rank had meant anything to them.

One eyebrow rose and she read the silent question in his expression: *What are you doing with my father's estate?*

Curtsy, a voice in her head shouted, *curtsy you chit!*

Lara curtsied as much as she could, acutely aware the clothes she wore belonged to Cezar's mother. "M-my lord, we were not expecting you until March."

Everybody in the room stopped whatever they were doing and sat like statues. *Disaster! We're all finished!* Lara's heart plummeted from behind her ribs to fall somewhere near her liver.

"Gentlemen, play on," Lord Cezar told the room,

"I shall join you presently. Meanwhile, enjoy my family's hospitality," then he turned to the ashen-faced Miss Jean and the face-burningly embarrassed Lara. "Ladies, meet me in my drawing room in five minutes."

"Yesmylord," Miss Jean and Lara said, running the words together.

"Schovajsa, you smell like sheep dip. Tomorrow you will bathe. For now, stay where you are."

"Sir," Schovajsa said, keeping his eyes down.

It was impossible to stop fidgeting as Lara and Jean stood in the cold drawing room, the furniture covered in dust sheets, the curtains drawn. Fine goose bumps spread over Lara's arms, and it wasn't from the cold, as her face burned with shame. Footsteps approached just as she was about to ask Miss Jean what punishment they might be in for.

When he walked in, Lara's breath stopped. Cezar looked magnificent. He'd changed into fresh clothes and had splashed water over his face and thick, brown hair. His wet eyelashes clumped together, creating long curtains around his deep blue eyes. Her gaze rested on his full lips. Something fluttered in her stomach, and it had nothing to do with her impending doom.

"Miss Jean, you may leave," he said.

The woman curtsied, headed to the door, then

paused, "My lord, do ye mean I'm to leave the estate, or just this room?"

"We have guests in the dining room, Miss Jean. Attend them."

Jean nodded and fled.

As the door closed, Lara stood alone in the darkened room with her former childhood friend. A friendship that had clearly come to an end. Her pulse hammered in her ears. The axe would fall soon.

"You've turned my family's estate into a gambling den," he said. A ridge formed between his eyebrows in concern, but the corner of his strong mouth quirked upwards. "And at this most magical time of year."

How did she read such a face? Was he enjoying this?

Confess! Confess everything and beg his forgiveness. Lara dropped to her knees and clasped her hands together over her bosom. "Please, Sir, it was all my idea. I dragged Miss Jean and Schovajsa into it. Punish me if you must, but they are innocent."

To make matters worse, a pin from her skirts loosened and the glass statue rolled onto the floor. In the dim light, the faerie's heart glowed a deep blue.

"What is this?" Cezar asked. In two strides he reached Lara's position. He grabbed the statue and marvelled at it.

Desperation sent her mind in a spin; Lara lunged forward and grabbed at his legs, pressing her body into to his flesh. Firm, warm flesh that sent strange sensations darting through her body, "Please, Sir, give it back."

"Steady on. I'm not casting you out. The gambling idea is a stroke of genius. There is so little else to do in winter. Aside from hide from marauding armies, although they appear to have moved on."

Shock fizzed through her body. Lara tilted her face to look at his, but her eyes couldn't look past the front of his breeches. Heat raced up her neck and face afresh, and she sprang away from him in newly discovered shock.

Cezar laughed and kept his gaze locked with hers as he held the statue, "Whatever this is, it's important to you, so I'm going to keep it for the time being."

"But you can't Sir. It doesn't belong to me, it belongs to—oooh!" She covered her mouth before she incriminated herself any further.

"Tell me, Lara, you have nothing to fear from me."

The way her name flowed from his lips did strange things to her insides, and she cursed the stays yet again for making it so hard to breathe. With a trembling sigh, she told him everything. The silver schlipps she'd stolen from the Comte to buy the statue from the witch, and the gambling sessions to pay the money back before the family returned in spring.

"You've left out one detail," Cezar said, the knot in his brows long gone, the amused quirk on his lips fixed in place, "What is the statue for?"

Repent, repent. Lara threw herself to the ground,

causing a cloud of dust to swirl around her. "Please forgive me."

"Get up." He sounded exasperated. As she began to rise, his eyes widened and Lara realized she must be showing an extraordinary amount of bosom. His voice grew thick and husky, "On second thoughts, stay exactly where you are…"

Dust swirled around her. Lara started coughing, making her whole body shake. Her tightly reigned bosom threatened to break free. Quickly she stood up and turned away. Not having to look at him made it easier for the words to come.

"The faerie will find my one true love."

"Will it now?"

"The witch promised."

Silence for a moment, then she heard a soft metallic creak and she turned to see him placing the statue in a safety box. Then he locked it with a key and placed the key in his pocket.

"I must have it!" Lara pleaded.

"And you will. But first you must pay back my father's money, which means you will work for me. Let us not keep our guests waiting, there's money to be made."

---

1. Respect the plütz, it dulls the brain and hastens drinkers along the road to disaster. Although some claim the journey there is quite delightful.

Chapter 3

lever Lara. Cezar mused as the gentleman played on through the afternoon.

Setting up a games house during winter was a spark of brilliance. Why hadn't he thought of it?

With four elder brothers, Cezar would receive little from his family estate. His father had suggested he buy a military commission, but that would mean he'd have to join one of the neighbouring armies and take on Napoleon. Not something he particularly wanted to do. Not at this time of year at any rate.

Another choice was to travel to the Americas and make his name there. But why risk a long journey at sea when he could just as easily gamble here and win—with Lara? The girl whose smile he couldn't erase from his memory.

The next luncheon - he was already planning that -

would have more guests, with more money too. Not everyone fled south for winter. He knew exactly which lords (and lads born on the wrong side of the bed) to invite. Perhaps there would be some nearby regiments only too keen for some levity to brighten their gloomy lives?

When his family returned, he'd have to find a new location, but the games would continue. Perhaps they would rent rooms in neighbouring Slaegal? Go to the customers rather than making the customers come to them? Ah, but that would add to the costs, and that's where Lara's clever plan really paid out. Everything the guests ate and drank came from the estate. They didn't even realize they were eating peasant food.

Playing cards and dice through the afternoon with his new guests, Cezar made sure he lost as many hands as he won. If his guests lost too much money, they might not come back.

It was such tremendous fun to have company in the otherwise empty estate.

The best game he had all afternoon was keeping Lara's hands away from his pocket where the key lay. Each time she approached with a tray of food for the guests, she'd surreptitiously slip her soft hand down near his leg. Each time he'd playfully slapped her away, their guests none the wiser.

As the rain closed in and the sun dipped low, it was time for their guests to depart so they could get home. Cezar bid them farewell and returned to the games room, where he found Lara cleaning the tables.

"Bravo," he made a bow, "You are so enterprising. If I'd known this is what you got up to while we were away, I would have stayed behind last winter."

Lara made another curtsey—in abridged form as her hands held trays of dirty plates, "No Sir. We've never done anything like this before I assure you."

Something kicked in Cezar's stomach as his gaze locked at her innocent, wide eyes, her soft pale face with pink cheeks and lips. My how she'd filled out these last few years.

"How much money did we make today?"

"Ten gold coins for entry, and an extra fifteen schlipps from house winnings, Sir. Everybody went away happy," she said, her eyes glistening in triumph.

Cezar grinned. "Lara, let us have more of these gatherings, and I will make sure you earn enough to repay the debt before my family return. How does that sound?"

"That is more than acceptable, Sir. And when am I to get the faerie back?"

Doubt flicked through Cezar and he reached into his pocket. To his relief, he found the key and held it up, "This remains with me, to ensure your compliance with our business activities, and your silence upon my family's return."

Three weeks and three highly successful gaming after-noons later, Lara had repaid only half her debt. During this time, every eligible bachelor in the land must have crossed the Comte of Wistringia's threshold. The sun struggled to rise before nine and plummeted by four. The silver lining to this early sunset meant some gamblers stayed too long at the tables, thus requiring a room overnight. They charged for that as well.

It was nearly Christmas, surely the witch would be wanting her faerie back so she too could head south to escape the freezing months ahead? But with the faerie's glowing heart locked away, Lara had no way of knowing who her true love could be. Many gentlemen had returned since that first day of cards, but some had not. What if her true love had come and gone and she'd missed her chance?

As she carried fresh towels to Mister Cezar's cham-ber, nagging doubt clawed at her mind. If the faerie had changed back to red, the witch would want it returned—and nobody who valued their life ever double-crossed a witch. Alas, the delicate statue remained sealed in a box and Cezar had the key.

Consumed with her thoughts, Lara walked into his chambers without knocking first, and nearly dropped her bundle. There stood Cezar, at his basin, nude from the waist up. Her pulse beat a tattoo inside her chest as she took in his bare form, that beautiful skin stretched over lean limbs and broad shoulders, the sprinkling of soft hair over his chest. It would be impolite to keep looking, although it took all her power to drag her eyes away. When she did, her glance alighted on the locked box and her breath hitched. Her faerie was inside.

"You may have taken over the drawing room, but my chamber is private," Cezar said, rounding on Lara. His broad naked chest made her feel like swooning. The swoon developed a spine the moment she saw the key, tied loosely around his neck on a leather strap. The metal glinted in the light as it bounced against his skin.

"I'm sorry Sir, I'm so sorry," Lara hastily backed out of the room and closed the door behind her.

As she walked down the hall, she heard Cezar's deep rumbling laugh echoing from his room. A smile formed on her lips as a plan to get back her faerie formed in her mind.

It was dark. Lara's stays pinched. Something she'd grown accustomed to as she tried not to make a sound while creeping down the hall in the middle of the night. The candle flickered strange shadows on the walls with each step she took towards Cezar's chamber.

Cre-e-e-e-eak.

The floorboard noise reverberated in Lara's ears,

along with the thump-thump-thump of her elevated heartbeat. The door to his room was closed; she turned the handle and winced as it too creaked in the stillness of night. To her immense relief it began to rain, the soft pattering on the roof and windows muffled her approach. Lara held her breath again as she stepped towards his bed and pulled back the curtain. There he was, the rugs pulled right up to his neck. One lean, hair-dusted leg hung over the side. His stern face looked serene, but most importantly, his eyes were closed.

She put the candle softly on the side table and dried her sweaty palms on her skirts. Then she carefully placed her hand under the covers, searching for the key around his neck.

"Thief!" he called out, grabbing Lara's wrist and pulling her onto the bed. Before Lara could scream, he tossed her onto her back, capturing the length of her body against his. "I have you now!"

In the candlelight, Lara could see his smile made entirely for sin.

"Please kiss me," Cezar said. "Just a kiss, nothing more."

"Just a kiss then," she agreed.

His lips crashed down on hers. Lara's eyes flew wide at the sensual onslaught. Something strange and wonderful flipped low in her belly. Her lids fell shut, surrendering to the pleasure. His mouth coaxed hers open. Her head told her to stop, but her body told her to take all the pleasure she could get. Cezar let go of her wrist and placed his hands either side of her body, holding himself against her, yet protecting her from his full weight.

With both hands free, Lara cupped her palms to his beautiful face, stroked his cheeks and ran her fingers through his thick hair. All the while those lips cast a spell on her, sending arrows of heat through her body.

"I want you, Lara," he kissed her lips, chin, neck and shoulders. His fingers moved to the laces on her clothes, where her breasts ached to break free.

The key hung between them, suspended around his neck on that thin piece of leather. She could reach out and snatch it away, yet right now, her hands had better things to play with.

"You are the devil," Lara said, yet all the while she wanted him, wanted his hands on her.

He chuckled as he nibbled at her earlobe, "Guilty as charged."

Nothing in her life had ever had this effect. A mixture of the soft yearning she felt when she cuddled wee Pavel, mixed with the giddy recklessness after a dram of plütz. It was both these things and more. Something strange and definitely addictive.

And dangerous.

Bells clanged in her head. This couldn't be happening, not like this. To him it would be nothing more than a romp in the night. But if things continued, Lara would give away the only bargaining chip she had to secure a palatable marriage. Born low, her family not from these parts, her options were limited enough.

Lara's eyes bolted open and her entire body turned rigid. "Stop! Please, I beg you, Sir. Stop!"

Immediately, but with a groan that sounded like frustration, he rolled to the side and covered his face. "I thought you'd come to me willingly?"

A single tear ran down Lara's face and she sat up on the bed, curling her knees up to her chest. She felt responsible for this—she had come to his room willingly enough, but not for the reason he'd suspected.

"It was a mistake to come here. I thought I could get the faerie back without your knowledge. I had not bargained on you being awake, or having other … desires."

"Lara, you are so very desirable. You came to my room in the dead of night, slipping your lovely hand under the rugs. What was I to think?"

Did he speak the truth, or did he merely want to satisfy his carnal urges?

"You are toying with me, Sir," Lara said, recovering some of her wits as she stepped away from the bed, "But you ask much too high a price, for something that is no more than a game to you. Sir, if there is any good in you at all, return me the faerie and let me go in peace."

With a sigh of resignation, he lifted the leather

strap over his head, and held the key out to Lara. "I would never ask anything of you, that you weren't prepared to give freely."

"Thank you, Sir," Lara said as she took the key, then made her way to the side table and unlocked the box. Her pulse leapt as she saw the faerie inside, unharmed. Then her hope sagged as she saw its heart—it glowed red. The witch wanted it back.

All was lost. Her true love had come and gone and she hadn't recognized him. Foolish, foolish, girl.

"Is everything in order?" Cezar asked.

"Yes, Sir, it is. But I am not. I must return the faerie tomorrow, and I am none the wiser as to the identity of my true love."

"I see."

"But I don't think you do, Sir. You are the son of a comte; you can find your mate at your leisure. I am no more than the milkmaid daughter of a nobody, and now my chance is gone!"

"Oh but Lara, you are so much more than that." He closed the distance between them, took her hand in his and kissed the inside of her wrist. The contact sent the most delicious fire through her system and she thought she might lose her mind. How easily she could fall for his hypnotic kisses.

"You have pretty words and a handsome face, Sir. But if I accept your advances, it will utterly ruin me. Please let me go."

The hand that held hers fell away, and Lara turned and walked out before he could see the tears falling down her cheeks.

Chapter 4

"It didn't work. I believe you should return the coins I paid you." Lara told the witch the next day, as she took her seat in the covered wagon.

"It did work," she protested, tucking the faerie safely away. "The enchanted faerie is never wrong. There are no refunds."

"But, it didn't tell me who my one true love was, like it was supposed to." To her immense shame, she burst into tears. She must be tired, what with all the tossing and turning last night, chasing sleep that would not come.

"It glowed purple and blue, did it not?"

"Yes but . . . then it got locked away and I didn't see which gentleman the faerie was glowing to, or for, or whatever. And it took ages to get it back and by then it was red."

"Hush, child. You have kept your end of the

bargain, and I have kept mine. I promise you, you have met your one true love."

It was a cold, wet walk back to the servants' quarters Lara shared with Miss Jean and Pavel. But when Lara returned, all their belongings were gone. They must have been dismissed, it was the only explanation. She'd refused Cezar last night, so this morning he must be throwing them all out.

"Well!" she huffed to the empty room, "You can throw me out, but there's no reason to take it out on Schovajsa or Miss Jean and wee Pavel."

Armed with a head full of steam and a heart full of bluster, Lara stomped into the big house. Wonderful cooking smells enveloped her senses as soon as she walked in.

Beef? Since when did they cook meat in the Comte's absence? Lara's heart sank at the implications—the entire family must be returning home for Christmas. Yet she hadn't earned nearly enough to repay the debt. Things could not get any worse!

In the kitchen she found Miss Jean, wee Pavel and another man Lara didn't recognize. Then she heard him speak. It was Schovajsa—what a difference a bath and a shave could make! They looked happy, not at all like they'd been given their marching orders.

"What's going on?" Lara asked, her head swirling in confusion.

"You'd best see Lord Cezar, he's in the games room," Jean basted the meat, avoiding eye contact with Lara.

To add to her confusion, Lara heard Miss Jean giggling as she walked away.

Right, let's get this over with. Lara took a deep breath and turned the handle to the games room. She found her nemesis sitting near the roaring fire, a deck of cards in his hands, a vacant chair opposite him.

When he looked up at her, Lara's heart thumped against her ribs. So handsome, yet when he smiled at her right now, it didn't quite reach his eyes. His face looked flushed, his brow furrowed.

"Please take a seat," he said, gesturing to the empty chair.

Lara did as instructed, breath hitching in her throat, pulse pounding in her ears.

"About last night …" he started.

"Sir. I understand you must dismiss me, but please do not punish Miss Jean and baby Pavel into the bargain. Or Schovajsa. They are good, obedient people, whereas I am wicked and deserve to be cast into hell."

To her astonishment, Cezar coughed and then smothered his hand over his face. But she could tell by the way his eyes crinkled that he was grinning behind his hand.

"I am an amusement, Sir, nothing more. Again, please send me on my way, but Miss Jean should remain here."

Cezar leaned forward and took Lara's hand, "I have no intention of dismissing Jean, Schovajsa, or your good self. Hear me out, and then you may speak. As you said last night, your true love may have come . . . and gone. Perhaps I may . . . present myself . . . as an alternative?"

Lara drew breath, making her stays pinch a little, but they didn't hurt anymore as she'd become used to them. She said nothing. Not that she was being particularly obedient, simply that no words would come. Was he proposing, or making a *proposition*?

Still no words came.

"Why don't we let the cards decide?" Cezar shuffled the deck and fanned them out. "If I pick the high card, you agree to marry me. If you pick the high card, you have your freedom."

The son-of-a-comte! The man she'd nearly lost her head and body to last night, wanted her for his wife, not his mistress! Well now, that changed everything!

Stunned into silence, Lara could only nod.

Cezar drew first, a smile split his face. The Queen of Hearts.

"I need you, Lara," Cezar said. "You are a breath of fresh air in this stuffy estate, and I love your spirit of enterprise. I never thought I would make a marriage offer to anyone, let alone for love. Yet I find myself doing exactly that. I love you Lara. I think I've loved you since we played in the fields together. Marry me. Together we can make our future and our fortune together. With your wonderful ideas and my connections."

The words, when they came, sounded thin and squeezed, "But your family would disinherit you."

"There is no inheritance, not for one born so low in the pecking order as I. Yet it is a blessing, as I can choose whom to marry. I choose you, if you will have me."

With shaking hands, Lara accepted the pack of cards and held them. Not shuffling, not fanning them out, just holding them as a block. The upturned Queen of Hearts that Cezar had drawn looked back at her and she understood. The faerie had led her to her one true love, and he was sitting before her. That's why she could smell meat cooking from the kitchen—Jean wasn't preparing for the master to return, she was preparing a celebration for them!

There was only one thing to do. She threw the rest of the cards into the fire and they burned brightly in the flames.

"Sir, I do not need to draw a card to decide my fate, as I find myself hopelessly in love with you and will gladly follow you anywhere."

Joy erupted on his face like a flame to saltpetre. Cezar leapt to his feet and pulled Lara into an embrace. He sealed their fate as he claimed her lips with his. For a moment, time stopped for the two of them, lost in their private universe. Then he broke away, although his gaze stayed locked with Lara's.

"You can come in now, Miss Jean, Schovajsa," Cezar said.

The door opened and the servants came in, with a tray of boiled eggs and milk to snack on. They also had a collection of ribbons in several hues.

"I know of your local custom of hand joining," Cezar said, accepting a broad, blue ribbon from the tray, "With Schovajsa and Jean here as witnesses, I declare my steadfast devotion and love for you, Kylara Novak, forsaking all others, until the gods take my body to the next world."

He placed the ribbon over their wrists. Then Schovajsa, looking clean and shiny and smelling like a spring meadow instead of a goat paddock, stepped forward and tied the first knot. Jean followed with another ribbon, which she knotted around their wrists, and stepped back to admire her handiwork.

Then Schovajsa selected another ribbon, but this time he turned to Miss Jean, "My dear, with witnesses and all, will ye have me?"

Lara blinked at the unfolding scene before her.

"Oh be off with ye," Jean batted his arm away— although not with much conviction, "I'm keeping my options open."

"But ye've got me baby in ye belly woman! And there's young Pavel too!"

Jean's face paled to the colour of milk. "I think I smell something burning," she blurted, and dashed to the kitchen. Schovajsa followed in pursuit.

Giggles erupted from Lara, then Cezar smothered her laugh with a newly minted kiss that sent flurries of desire all the way to her toes.

When he broke away, Cezar gave Lara a look of such longing she felt like her insides could melt under the intensity, "I like the idea of my baby in your belly. Lots of babies, all as clever as you."

"And all of them as handsome as you, Sir," Lara kissed him with all the love she had in her.

"My dear Lara."

"Yes, Sir?"

"Don't you think it's time you called me Cezar?"

Lara snuggled herself against him, bathed in the combined glow of the fire and his warmth, "Yes, Cezar. I do."

As they stood together, united, Lara knew with a bone-deep certainty she had found her true love and her future. She would call him Cezar as he had asked. But sometimes, when they were alone together, she'd quite enjoy calling him 'Sir'.

Make Your Own Brugelwürst

A favourite recipe, handed down for generations. Everybody loves it, until they see how it's made.

Ingredients:

- 500g chicken or other poultry livers
- 2 or 3 onions
- clove of garlic (or more, depending on how much you love garlic and don't like people)
- 10 peppercorns – soaked and plump so they puree beautifully later
- I cup of chopped leek – the green part from the top

- I cup chopped spring onion / green onion
  – the green part from the top
- 1 tablespoon of tarragon
- 1 tablespoon of mixed herbs – whatever
  you have in the pantry or garden will do
- 3 tablespoons of butter
- More melted butter for later

Method:

1. Grab a wooden chopping board and a
   super-sharp knife. Chop the onions in half
   and lay them face-down on the board. Let
   the juices soak into the board while you
   prepare everything else. You will thank me
   in a moment.
2. On that same wooden board, squash the
   garlic clove/s under the widest part of the
   knife.
3. Put the butter, garlic and livers in the
   saucepan, on very low heat (you don't want
   to burn the butter) and cook away. Make
   sure the extraction fan is sucking
   everything out of your house. Open the
   windows.
4. Add all the herbs and other ingredients
   except the onion.
5. Come back to the onion now and peel the
   skin away and slice the onion. Are you

crying? You are not crying. The juices have soaked into the board instead of your face. You are welcome. Also, never use this board again for anything other than onions. Or garlic.

6. When everything is soft and cooked and the livers fall to bits when you poke them with a spoon, it's time to transfer everything into a blender and puree the lot until it's lovely and smooth. (For a chunkier Brugelwürst, hold some of the livers back from the blending and add them back in when pouring into ramekins. I love the word ramekins. It implies that somewhere there is a very big Mama Ramek and these are her babies.)

7. Pour the mix into ramekins, leaving at least 1cm from the top.

8. Melt butter and gently pour over the top of the Brugelwürst to form a seal. Let them cool on the bench for a little while, then transfer to the refrigerator. The butter will harden and form a solid seal, keeping it fresh. It will also hold back the smell from infesting your refrigerator. You are extra welcome.

Serve cold with toast triangles or squares (wars have been fought over whether toast should be cut on the diagonal or vertical. I don't want to cause offence. Maybe it's best to use crackers instead?)

Enjoy.

Nutritional value:

Brugelwürst is very low in carbohydrate and fibre, high in delicious fats, protein and the Vitamin B family. It's very high in Vitamin A. Best eaten with multigrain toast to balance things out.

Make Your Own Fried Cheeseballs

IF YOU'VE NEVER HAD FRIED CHEESEBALLS, DO
YOU EVEN BRUGEL?

A hot, fat, salted snack, perfect for the colder months.
The ultimate street food from Venzelemma.

Ingredients:

- 250 grams grated cheese medley - a good
  melty type like mozarella or havarti works
  well, mixed with something a more bitey
  like cheddar and parmesan.

- 1 cup flour.
- Seasoning of your choice - salt and pepper, curry powder, chicken stock powder, have fun!
- 2 eggs, beaten.
- 1 cup milk.
- 2 cups of breadcrumbs - crushed cornflakes make excellent breadcrumbs.
- Vegetable oil with a high smoke point. Peanut oil has the highest smoke point, but watch out for allergies.

Method:

1. Grab three bowls and make a production line - fill one with flour and seasoning, one with the beaten egg and milk, and the third with the breadcrumbs.
2. In another bowl - we're up to four now, so there's some washing up to do later - grate your cheeses and mix together.
3. Grab spoonfuls of cheese and squish into ball shapes, not too big or they'll be too hard to eat. You want them a nice small size that will go straight into your mouth in one go.
4. Roll your cheeseballs in the flour, tap excess flour away, then roll in the egg mix, then roll in the breadcrumbs.

5. Whoa, you're going to need another bowl to place the assembled cheeseballs. Hope you have a good dishwasher.

6. You're not going to believe this, but you'll need yet another bowl now - because you're going to need a clean bowl to place the cooked cheeseballs - don't put cooked food back in the same bowl as raw food, that's a really good way to end up in Venzelemma hospital.

7. Put a few layers of paper towel in this bowl, to soak up the excess oil.

8. Pour oil into a pan - 5cm deep - and get the temperature up to 180 Celsius. Using a slotted metal spoon, carefully place the cheeseballs into the oil. Stand back while it all bubbles and splatters.

9. When the cheeseballs are golden brown, use your metal spoon to lift them out and put them in the clean bowl.

10. Enjoy your hot snack. Serve with your favourite dips in yet more bowls. Enjoy cleaning up the mess!

11. Maybe next time you might buy them from the street vendor instead?

Nutritional Value:
Pffffft!

Author's Notes

I hope you've had the most wonderful time in Brugel. I certainly had a ball translating and re-interpreting these Brugelish fairytales. They have a timeless quality about them which makes them resonate in the modern world.

Fairytales are some of the oldest forms of story-telling. Many had macabre warnings suitable for the times they were told. Stick to the paths, watch out for wolves, that sort of thing. In so many of the tales, the protagonist died at the end. Often miserably.

Often the stories were twisted or misheard in the retellings, or became corrupted in translation. One thing that has always confused me is the concept of 'letting down your hair' from the story of Rapunzel. It would have been very difficult, if not impossible, for a young woman to grow hair long enough for a suitor to climb up the side of a tower. (Yes, I know, it's a fairy-tale. But also, how did she go to the toilet?)

The concept of a girl being locked away by a witch sounds much more like an heartsick teenager being kept away from boys by her panicked parents. Before wigs were invented, or affordable to non-royals, people would have tied up their hair with cloth and tucked it under their hats. When people were alone together, they would 'let down their hair', and possibly their inhibitions.

People often ask writers, "Where you you get your ideas from?" The answer? Everywhere. Writers are always capturing and storing information because that's how our brains work. I love going to weekly trivia nights, because my head is filled with obscure information, and it's a handy place to find more. A recent question prompted a story in this very collection:

"What's the Guiness World Record for the most number of live births from one woman?"

The answer was 69 (from one woman!) and our host shared this after revealing the answer.

According to Guiness World Records, the most prolific mother was the wife of Feodor Vassilyev (b. 1707 – c.1782) a peasant from Shuya, Russia. In 27 confinements, she gave birth to 16 pairs of twins, seven sets of triplets and four sets of quadruplets.

The trivia host and I instantly noticed a huge problem with this information. What was THE MOTHER'S name? She was the one spending her adult life pregnant, birthing and breastfeeding, but she's only referred to as 'the wife'. Thanks, patriarchy!

It got me thinking about a woman with so many children, and although it is theoretically possible, the lack of hygiene and nutrition of the times makes this an almost impossible task. Wouldn't it be more likely that people were taking their unwanted babies to this family? Word gets around that somebody will take them in and look after them … it wouldn't take much.

Added to this, the location – Shuya - which sounds like shoe, doesn't it?

Which instantly makes one think of the nursery rhyme:

There was an old woman who lived in a shoe.
She had so many children, she didn't know what to do.
She gave them some broth without any bread;
Then whipped them all soundly and put them to bed.

Why would she whip them? This sounds like the behaviour of somebody working in an orphanage, overwhelmed by the workload!

A little googling later, it appears that the first publication of this rhyme was in a 'Mother Goose' collection from 1794. Plenty of time for this story from Shuya, Russia, to grow wings across Europe and take on a life of its own.

I hope you've had the most wonderful time in Brugel with these charmingly batty characters. I thank you by the Brugelish bucketload (the buckets are bigger in Brugel) for purchasing this book.

I doubly thank you in advance for recommending this book to your friends.

Please leave a review on your website of choice. Every time a reader leaves a review, a snowgoat gets their horns.

Triple thanks, Ebony.

Acknowledgments

So many wonderful people contributed directly or indirectly to the making of this book. First of all I'd like to thank the people of Saigon in the 1950s for creating the Bánh mì, the ongoing consumption of which directly influenced many stories within these pages. I'm sure my blood now tests positive for coriander, hoisin sauce and pork crackling.

To my wonderful writing friends in The Saturday Ladies' Bridge Club. You are my people! Thank you for providing a nurturing and encouraging space. Thank you for kicking me up the backside when required, which is often.

Another essential team I must thank is The House of Progress, whose members scare me a little (ok, a lot) with their incredible work ethic and talent. Progressers, you delight and fill me with wonder every day. Scarily, you also knew I was Hufflepuff even before I did.

To Heather, who has always been delightfully bonkers and gives me my best material. Thank you!

To Rod and Janet, for being so supportive, long after the novelty of writing novels wore off.

To my extended family of in-laws, out-laws and in-case-of-emergencies … thank you for making this try-hard try that bit harder each time.

To Stephen and Josh, forever and ever and ever and ever and I hope I never stop embarrassing you. It's my JOB!

Also by Ebony McKenna

The Ondine series (in reading order)

The Summer of Shambles

The Autumn Palace

The Winter of Magic

The Spring Revolution

A Brugel Fairytale Treasury

Other young adult novels

1916-ish

Robyn and the Hoodettes

The Girl & The Ghost - RWA 2018 RuBY winner for Romantic Book of the Year

Short stories

Dangerous Honesty (from *Dangerous Boys* anthology)

I'm Still Here (from *The Hauntings of Livingstone Hall* anthology)

The Woman Who Saved The World And Was Hated For It

Non-Fiction author guides

The First Three Chapters

Edit Your Own Romance Novel

Edit Your Own Young Adult Novel

Get Your Book Into Australian Libraries

About the Author

Ebony McKenna is the author of the four-part Ondine series, about a girl whose pet ferret starts talking with a Scottish accent. (The ferret is really a man who offended a witch, and Ondine will do whatever she can to break the spell.)

She has lived all over Victoria, including Lorne, Maldon, Narre Warren and Ballarat. But not in that order.

These days she lives in suburban Melbourne and is busy dreaming up more adventures. If you've enjoyed reading this book, please consider leaving a review.

Come and say hello on 'the socials'
www.ebonymckenna.com
author@ebonymckenna.com
facebook.com/EbonyMcKenna
instagram.com/ebonymckennawrites

Turn the page to read the first chapter of the book that started it all, *The Summer of Shambles*.

The Summer of Shambles: Ondine
Book 1

T his is a great story, and like a good many great stories before it, it begins with a teenage girl. Her name is Ondine de Groot and she is fifteen. She has long dark hair past her shoulders, which is neat for about five minutes before it gets messy and stringy.

Her eyes are dark brown and pretty, except when she's rolling them. She also adores small animals, of which you will hear more in a moment.

Ondine's story began exactly twelve years ago today, in a place called Brugel. [1] It's a pretty country in Eastern Europe, which is well known for its old buildings. [2]

On the day this story began, Ondine was nearing the end of her time at Psychic Summercamp. As the name suggests, Psychic Summercamp was a place for students to spend their summer holidays developing their psychic and other extra-sensory skills. In some countries, students spend their holidays at adventure camp, fat camp or mathletics. In Brugel, they do things differently.

Back to Ondine. She was in a dormitory with three other girls (who were asleep on account of it being so early in the morning) and she awoke with a jolt.

"Saturn's rings! It's six o'clock! I've slept through the astral projection exam." Ondine sat up and pushed the covers away. The bed's throw blanket fell to the floor, smothering the furry black ferret that lay curled up beneath.

"Melody, wake up," she said, nudging the sleeping girl in the bunk above her. "What happened in the astral exam?"

It took Melody a few more nudges to wake up. Yawning, she swiped her mousy-blonde hair from her face, rubbed the sleep from her eyes and inspected it, then stopped as she realized she had an audience.

"Ah, sorry." Melody looked embarrassed as she blinked herself awake. "What's going on, what time is it? The sun isn't even up." The psychic lessons didn't seem to have worked very well on her either.

"Shh, you'll wake the others," Ondine said. "Now, quick, what happened in the astral?"

"I . . . I don't know. I must have slept through it!" Melody's face crumpled and she made ready to cry. "I'm going to fail, aren't I?"

"Don't worry, I'll fail more than you." As Ondine looked around the room, she spotted the handle of her suitcase poking out from under her bed. It gave her an idea. "This entire thing is a waste of time, and a waste of our summer holidays. We're supposed to be having fun with boys and falling in love, not studying. I'm going to run away to home."

A great many girls of Ondine's age would love to run away from home, but Ondine was the other way around. She'd had it up to here (hold your hand at eyebrow level) with the whole psychic thing and knew it was time to quit.

And another thing, how was she supposed to have fun and meet cute boys if she spent her school holidays in another kind of school?

While Melody watched the door for teachers, Ondine packed up her clothes and her gimgaws and doohickie whatsits and zipped the case closed. [3]

"Shouldn't you tell Mrs Howser you're leaving?" Melody asked.

"Pfft. She's the psychic one, why should I bother?" Ondine looked at the sleeping forms of her remaining roommates. "You can tell the other two when they wake up."

"How will you get home?" Melody asked.

Valid question. Psychic Summercamp was located on the outskirts of Brugel's capital city, Venzelemma, and Ondine's family lived right over on the other side.

"There's a bus stop down the end of the street, so

I'll take that to central station. Then I'll get the train the rest of the way home." Ondine sounded pleased with her plan as she lifted the faux-fur-throw off the ferret and folded it into a messy rectangle-ish shape on the end of her bed.

The throw, not the animal. Ferrets don't fold so well.

"What about Shambles?" Melody asked, looking at the sleeping animal on the ground.

Oh dear. Ondine hadn't given much thought to the ferret, because she didn't think the creature should be coming with her. Ondine was more your fluffy kitten-y type of girl, so she hadn't given much attention that morning to the long and skinny bundle of black. Turning up at home, unannounced, before Summercamp finished would give her family enough of a fright. Turning up unannounced with a weasel in her hands might finish her mother right off.

"He's a sweet thing, and he's really taken to you." Melody's eyes were bright with possibilities.

"You're right," Ondine agreed.

During the weeks at camp, Ondine and Shambles the ferret had become unlikely buddies. He'd turned up one day and made himself at home, following Ondine about. [4] He'd even come to classes with her. The thought of abandoning the little fella to the craziness of Summercamp and Mrs Howser made something twist in her tummy. Probably guilt. A bit of hunger too.

Then Shambles the ferret woke up, spun around a few times and stood up on his hind legs, looking like an elongated, begging puppy. If puppies had pointy noses, long whiskers and sharp teeth.

"And nobody else got a pet while they were here," Melody said. "You were really lucky."

Hmmm, what to do? It didn't sit right with her conscience to leave him.

"I'll take him with me and find him a good home," Ondine said, scooping up the creature and tucking him into the crook of her arm. "Shambles, you're going to have to behave yourself or I'll leave you on the bus." It was her way of trying to sound stroppy. The little fella was pretty cute once you got to know him.

So that's how Ondine came to leave Psychic Summercamp on that warm summer's morning, with a ferret wrapped around her neck like a scarf and the scent of geraniums and lavender in her nostrils as she walked along the flower-studded footpath to the bus stop. [5]

The wind blew her hair in wild directions, whipping at her lips and eyes. There was nothing she could do to prevent it; she needed both hands to carry her heavy case. Not even a spare hand for Shambles – he hung on to her collar.

It wasn't until Ondine got off the bus and reached

Venzelemma's crowded central train station that the ferret spoke.

"Thank gooniss for tha–, I'm all bumpy and broke," Shambles said with a deep Scottish accent, then climbed on to her head to get a better view. "Progress! The train'll be here in a minute. When we get tae yer hoose we can eet, I'm fair starven."

Ondine gasped and dropped her case on the platform in shock. Because, make no mistake about it, there was definitely a man's voice coming from the ferret. Sure, summer was all about having fun and meeting boys, but not this kind!

Quickly, she found a place to sit down, then hauled Shambles into her hands to have a good look at him, all the time wondering if she'd gone a bit . . . funny.

"I've lost my mind," Ondine said. A furtive look around told her nobody else was paying them any attention. The station was full of grey-looking people heading off to work for the day, completely unaware of the teenage girl with scruffy brown hair holding a black ferret.

"Nae ye havnae, but ye can hear me," Shambles added in his thick brogue. "Looks like somethin' rubbed off at Summercamp."

Ondine rolled her eyes. "Ma will be so pleased. All that gypsy blood in my veins and all I can do is talk to rodents."

"I'm nae rodent, ye bampot, I'm a ferret.

Completely different. Right then, hae comes the loco. Let me at yer neck." [6]

"But . . . but!" Ondine's brain turned to slurry as she tried to make sense of this talking animal. All the while heated embarrassment roared up her neck and face.

"No backing out now, lassie. I'm coming with ye. Now grab the case and on we get. And upon my honour, I promise to behave."

What could she do? It was still such a shock that her new furry friend could talk. And why could she only hear him now? At that moment the train pulled in and Ondine had no more time for prevaricating. [7]

It was a tense ride home on the train, what with the uncomfortable wooden seats, a talking ferret wriggling about her neck and passengers giving her very strange looks. As soon as the engine arrived at her home station, Ondine grabbed Shambles away from her throat and put him on her shoulder.

His little paws reached up to the top of her head. He stretched and had a good look around.

"Oh, so ye live in this part of town, how very la-de-dah! No wonder yer parents have money tae pish away on psychic dafties."

By this point you may have formed the opinion that Shambles was not your run-of-the-mill ferret, and you'd be right. You may have also formed the opinion

that he's saucy and cheeky, and you'd be right there

too. But if you think he's nothing but trouble, you're wrong, although he does give that impression.

As keen as she was to race home, Ondine waited for the train to clear the station before she stepped off the end of the platform to walk across the tracks, looking both ways to make sure no other trains were coming. The pedestrian overpass would have been safer, but it was closed to the public until the official opening.

"Pinch me, I'm dreaming," Shambles said as he noted the direction Ondine was taking him. "The girl lives in a pub!"

The ferret spoke the truth. Ondine's parents ran a hotel and public bar on the main road in a pretty swanky part of Venzelemma. Three floors tall and painted bright blue and white, the hotel towered over the neighbourhood. Even the newer buildings looked like old buildings to help them blend in.

The Station Hotel prided itself on being a family business, where everyone pitched in and helped. Not yet old enough to serve alcohol in the bar, Ondine worked in the dining room and helped out behind the scenes. A lot.

Most people think if your parents run a restaurant, you eat delicious five-course meals every night.

You don't.

Ask anyone what it's really like and they'll tell you it's nothing but work. Washing dishes, ironing table-cloths, cleaning the floors, chopping wood for the fire, keeping the fire going all night, preparing food. Look, the list just goes on and on.

But for Ondine, working at home with her parents appealed more than howling at the moon or looking for omens in tea leaves or reading palms or any other great wastes of time that sucked away her precious summer holidays.

"Wait up, we cannae just walk in. Yer mother will fair faint," Shambles said, holding on to Ondine's shoulder.

That made Ondine stop for a moment and think about her plan of action.

"She'll be glad to see me," she said. "Although I don't know what she'll make of you. She's not the pet kind."

"I'm nobody's pet!" Shambles clenched his paws on his hips in frustration. "And dinnae tell no one about finding a new home for me, either. Yer the first person who's heard me in scores of years, mebbe more. I've lost count. I need ye tae stick around and help me, because I think I'm losing my social skills." [8]

Laughter caught in Ondine's throat. It had been a trying morning to say the least, and she wasn't used to lugging heavy things for long distances. Plates piled high with food were fine, because they only needed carrying from the kitchen to the dining-room tables. Heavy suitcases were another matter entirely.

"Are all ferrets like you? I mean, how come you can talk?"

"Because I'm nawt a real ferret. I'm Hamish McPhee, but I offended a witch and she turned me thus. I've bin like this for years. Powerful magic it was and all. Haven't a gray hair on me. Thank gooniss she used a staying spell."

Ondine's eyes widened in surprise. "You offended a witch? Wow!"

"Aye. She took it badly."

"You must have done something really awful to her." Her mind reeled as she wondered what sort of offensive thing might make a witch turn a regular man into a weasel. A regular man! Ondine's memory leapt back to her time in Summercamp, when she'd allowed Shambles to sleep in her dorm. Well, that was before she'd known what he really was. Now that she did know, there'd be no more of that!

"Aye, and I'm deeply ashamed," Shambles admitted.

"What did you do then? And is this witch about to descend on me and demand the return of her familiar?" [9]

"I'm no familiar! They're silly animals turned into fat-belly pets. I'll have ye remember I'm a regular man living in reduced circumstances."

"You're stalling. What did you do?"

"Aw, I was a right neep. [10] I was supposed tae partner her at a debutante ball. Ye know the ones, where the girls get all dolled up and look like brides?

And then they get presented to some fancy-pants man, like a mayor or a duke."

"It must have been a while ago. Hardly anyone does a deb any more."

"This girl took it real serious-like. And I didnae. I wasnae yer ideal partner, on account of the fact I had ma first taste of plütz that night." [11]

His tone told Ondine he felt truly sorry for his actions, and she started to feel a bit sorry for him in return.

By now they'd reached the back door. Ondine fished around in her pockets for her key and made ready to let them in. The smell of fried breakfast foods wafted from the kitchen windows, making her tummy rumble.

"Aw, breakfast. I could murder some big fatty sausage," Shambles said, his tongue licking the fur around his mouth in anticipation.

"You're stalling," Ondine said. "Tell me what happened, and then we'll have food."

"Ooooh, listen to ye! All grown up and sophisti-cated, like," Shambles teased, then Ondine stared daggers at him and his voice dropped to a sombre tone. "I didn't know she was a real witch, otherwise I wouldnae called her one. But she was getting snippy with me, so I ducked off and had some more plütz. It's like peaches and rocket fuel that stuff, and I've nawt touched it since. Then she got really pished with me when I stepped on her feet and fell over. I ripped the lacy bit at the bottom of her skirt and then she got really mad. She called me pond scum. I called her a witch. She looked like her head might explode. She said, 'You're damn right I'm a witch. And you're nothing better than a low-down weasel,' and then she said I could stay like that."

"Wow. And she turned you into a ferret, right there in front of everyone?"

"Naw, she turned me into a donkey! Of course she turned me into a ferret! She was fair affronted."

Ondine gaped at him.

"Ferrets are smaller than weasels, but we're the same family, so maybe I am a low-down weasel after all. But between us, I prefer ferret."

Ondine giggled. "I think she did the right thing. Debutante balls take a lot of organizing, and a lot of rehearsals. I think you should apologize to this poor girl as soon as possible. Then you might be yourself again." The thought of Shambles becoming himself made her wonder what he might look like if he were a real man again? His accent alone made her grin.

Opening the back door, the pungent odour of fried meats and old beer greeted them.

"Aww, that's the good stuff." Shambles took a noisy sniff.

"Ondine! What are you doing home?" her mother called out from the hallway.

"Hi, Ma, you look great. Have you lost weight? I love your hair." Her mother looked as plump as ever, but her new burgundy-brown hairdo skimmed her face and made her look thinner. Flattery ought to put her in a good mood. Just to be on the safe side, Ondine adopted what she hoped was a pleading look on her face. "I . . . I got homesick so I came back."

Ma stopped mid-stride, mouth open, when she saw the ferret on her daughter's shoulder. "Heavens above! What is that?" She pointed to the ferret with one hand, while the other patted the ample bosom above her heart, as if the beating organ might leap from her chest.

It called for quick thinking on Ondine's part, because her mother could be either furious or happy about the situation.

"He's really tame. Please, Ma, let me keep him?"

But Shambles was having none of it. "That's the one!" he cried out, finally finding his voice. He scurried down the back of Ondine's vest. "That's the witch!"

Footnotes:

1: One of the dozens of former Eastern Bloc countries, Brugel is mostly famous for three things. It has the only hexagonal flag in the world. Its main export is plütz, which is a tasty yet highly volatile vodka made from peaches. It has also never won the Eurovision Song Contest.

2: From a strategic point of view, Brugel was so

insignificant during World War Two that neither the Allies nor the Axis bothered to bomb it. This is why so many of its old buildings are still standing.

3: This was during the enormous gimgaw craze, so everyone had them. You won't find them now though.

4: She'd found him face-deep in her secret stash of Brugelwürst sausage, a local delicacy.

5: The flowers did their best to mask the smell of the ferret, but the ferret easily overpowered them.

6: Bampot is a silly person. A Daftie. Gets low grades at school and later in life rarely earns more than minimum wage.

7: Venzelemma is home to one of the oldest elektrichka train fleets in Europe. Their sparse interiors and spine-jarring wooden bench seats evoke equal amounts of old world nostalgia and sciatica. Most physiotherapists in Brugel are located within hobbling distance of train stations.

8: Pure denial. Shambles lost his social skills years ago.

9: A familiar is an animal form of supernatural spirit, who aids a witch in performing magic. Sometimes they're helpful, but in most cases they're useless. Have you ever seen a cat fetch the morning newspaper? Vacuum the floor? Make breakfast? Exactly.

10: Neep. Short for turnip.

11: Plütz is Brugel's number one alcoholic export. It is made from fermented peaches, is 32 per cent proof and is the main ingredient in divorce proceedings.

To read the entirety of *The Summer of Shambles*, join Ebony's author newsletter for a free ebook copy. Go to www.ebonymckenna.com and follow the links.

BOOK ONE IN THE HIGHLY ACCLAIMED SERIES

THE SUMMER OF SHAMBLES

AN ONDINE NOVEL

EBONY McKENNA

BOOK TWO IN THE HIGHLY ACCLAIMED SERIES
THE AUTUMN PALACE
AN ONDINE NOVEL
EBONY McKENNA

BOOK THREE IN THE HIGHLY ACCLAIMED SERIES
THE WINTER OF MAGIC
AN ONDINE NOVEL
EBONY McKENNA

BOOK FOUR IN THE HIGHLY ACCLAIMED SERIES
THE SPRING REVOLUTION
AN ONDINE NOVEL
EBONY McKENNA